THEATRE GHOST

THEATRE GHOST

Sarah A. Combs

ISBN-13: 9781535331593
ISBN-10: 1535331593
Library of Congress Control Number: 2016911764
CreateSpace Independent Publishing Platform
North Charleston, South Carolina

For theatre kids everywhere

Prologue

A ghost may come; for it is a ghost's right.

—WILLIAM BUTLER YEATS, "ALL SOULS' NIGHT"

An old man with a shock of white hair closed the filing cabinet, finished for the day. He pulled on a worn cardigan sweater. He could only fasten the top; the bottom button had been missing for years. His wife used to replace his lost buttons.

The man walked out of the backstage office and onto the stage. Crossing to a bank of levers on the wall, he grasped the largest and pulled it down. The theatre went dark. The only remaining light came from a single lightbulb surrounded by a wire cage, mounted on top of a pole. The man looked out at the theatre, gazing at the threadbare seats, memories flooding back to him. In its day, it had been magnificent.

He sighed and started back to the office. Halfway toward the wings, he stopped.

Voices.

But there shouldn't be anyone in the building. The theatre had been closed for decades. He himself had received the key only a month ago from the mayor so that he could begin researching the theatre's history.

The voices grew louder; they sounded garbled and unintelligible. Suddenly, a green circle of light reflected onto the stage floor in front of him. Startled, the man looked up. A small orb bobbed around over his head. He took in a sharp breath. With trembling hands, he rubbed his watery eyes and looked again. The green oval hovered and then moved slowly from side to side.

"What the hell?"

Abruptly, the orb darted into the house, zooming over the rows of seats, crisscrossing back and forth from the orchestra level to the balcony. Were his eyes playing tricks on him? Maybe he was too old to be working in the theatre again.

The light zoomed to a theatre box, slowed, and seemed to settle into a seat. There it remained, teasing him.

He stared at the green light illuminating the theatre box, trying to understand what his eyes were seeing, but his mind wasn't accepting. There, in the box usually reserved for important people, sat a man wearing an old-fashioned dark suit, perched as if he were watching a show. But this was impossible! The theatre had been empty—it *was* empty!

"Who's there?" he squeaked. Then he bravely raised his voice and yelled at the man, "Who are you?"

His voice echoed in the vacant hall. The shadows on the walls cast by the single lightbulb were moving, dancing, performing. The green orb of light rose up again, revolved, and picked up speed. It was racing straight toward him. Stumbling backward, he cried out, "*What* are you?"

The strange man in the theatre box remained motionless as the green light kept coming.

Paralyzed, the old man knew he should run, but fear kept him rooted to the stage. The caged light flickered once, and the theatre blacked out.

Don't let us make imaginary evils,
when you know we have so many real ones to encounter.

—OLIVER GOLDSMITH

A lden Proctor disentangled herself from the sheets, rolled over, and looked around her new room. The bright sun had awoken her. Their house, like most on Duke Street, was a brick Cape style with funny dormer windows that stuck out of the slanted roof. Alden and her mom had moved to Michigan two weeks ago. Had it only been two weeks? It seemed longer. She missed the brownstone they had lived in on Manhattan's Upper West Side. The apartment had originally belonged to her grandfather.

Duke Street was tranquil and lazy compared to her bustling previous one. When she'd first arrived, Alden had explored the neighborhood on her bike. She had watched other kids on her block with curiosity but hadn't approached them. In return, they'd ignored her.

A light breeze blew through her bedroom window. New York City sirens, car horns, and construction jackhammers were absent from the early-June morning. Pulling herself out of bed, she tugged down her pajama top, self-consciously covering her rolls of belly fat.

The walls of Alden's bedroom were adorned with Broadway show posters and ticket stubs. CDs of show recordings and souvenir programs were fondly organized on her bookshelves. On her dresser sat a framed picture of herself and Grandpa Charlie, their arms encircling each other, and their cheeks pressing together. Big smiles. The picture had been taken last fall after her eighth-grade debate against another New York middle school. Her team had won, and afterward, Grandpa Charlie had hugged her.

"Well done, Alden," he had said, slapping her raised palm. "Grand job, just grand."

Her mom had kissed her, her face bright with pride, her cheek wet against Alden's.

Alden picked up the photograph. The grief had dulled, but only a little. Shortly after the funeral, her mom had found a new job in Smithfield. Alden had welcomed the move, hoping it would be a new beginning for both of them.

Her grandpa had been a Broadway producer. Ever since she could remember, he had taken her to the theatre. He had invested in different types of productions, but Alden loved musicals the most. When she was little, she'd sit in the dark theatre next to her grandfather, just riveted by the color and light, the costumes, and scenery. As she aged, she became enamored with the dancers. Actually, she envied them. When Alden was alone, she'd listen to soundtracks and dance around, pretending she was in a show. Her Broadway fantasy never left her bedroom, though.

Her grandfather had had great success but also his share of flops. "It's a gamble," he'd tell her. "I like the risk. Besides, if I play it safe, where's the adventure?" Alden wished she could be more like him.

A loud knock on the door startled her.

"Hey—ya plan on getting up anytime today?"

Alden smiled. She liked Cleo's teasing sarcasm. "Yeah, I'm coming."

"Your mom wants you to meet her at the theatre for lunch. There's time for a bike ride before you go."

Cleo, a college student her mom had hired to help around the house, was majoring in culinary arts at the state university in Smithfield. She was teaching Alden to cook and trying to get her to focus on better eating habits. Every evening, they sampled one of her culinary concoctions.

Alden stuffed her cell phone into the pocket of her bathrobe and went downstairs to the kitchen. She was hungry, craving cinnamon buns. But Cleo had put homemade granola, low-fat milk, and a basket of strawberries on the table. Alden wrinkled her nose distastefully but grabbed a bowl and spoon—anything to silence her growling stomach.

"I've gotta run over to campus and register for the fall semester. Text me when you leave, okay?" Cleo grabbed her keys and started out the back door. "I'll be back later this afternoon."

"What's for dinner?" Alden asked.

"Grilled lake trout with tomatoes and basil."

"Why not grilled cheeseburgers?" Alden complained.

Ignoring her, Cleo said, "You can help me with the food prep. Don't forget to check in with me."

"Are we gonna have dessert?"

In answer, the screen door banged shut behind Cleo.

After she'd eaten, Alden showered and pulled on a pair of shorts, an oversized T-shirt, and sandals. Then, completing her mom's mental checklist, she locked the house, sent a text to Cleo, and retrieved her bike from the garage. Pedaling down Duke Street, she turned onto Main and then paused at the next corner. On impulse, she eased onto Oakdale, a section of the neighborhood she hadn't explored yet. The street didn't look anything like Alden's block. The houses were unkempt, the paint peeling, and the bushes overgrown. As she rode farther, Alden came across an old farmhouse with a large wraparound porch. Sections of the house's siding were missing, exposing pieces of tarpaper and insulation. The porch roof was jacked up with wooden supports:: the lattice was dirty and broken. A collection of old tires and lawn mowers lay under the trees, and pieces of machinery were strewn around the yard. One of the trees had a hand-drawn sign nailed to it:

Lawn Mowor Repair
Ask Inside

Below the lettering was a picture of a man repairing a machine. Alden looked more closely. The man was muscular, his face rugged, and he had a detailed tattoo on his bicep. The sign was artistic and drawn expertly.

Alden's front wheel hit the curb with a jolt. Laughter came from the porch.

"What'sa matter? Can't ya ride?"

Somehow Alden managed to stay on her bike, but heat crept up her neck and spread to inflame her cheeks. Looking up at the porch, she saw two boys. One had scraggly brown hair and wore a muscle shirt. He didn't have muscles, but Alden surmised that he liked to think he did. The second boy was shorter and had straight blond hair pulled back into a tight ponytail.

Muscle Shirt taunted, "Hey, did you hear me? You better go back to training wheels." Both boys laughed and smacked each other as Alden struggled to turn her bike around.

"Maybe if you ride around the block a few more times, you'll lose a few pounds!"

They laughed even louder. Ponytail said, "Good one, Raccoon."

So Muscle Shirt had a name—a furry, disease-carrying varmint.

"Ever hear of Jenny Craig?" continued Ponytail.

Instantly the tears came. Blinking them away, Alden lashed out, "Well, why don't you learn to spell?"

"Huh?" said Ponytail, looking over at his muscle-free friend.

Ponytail boy was obviously an idiot.

"Your sign," Alden said, clenching her teeth. "It's spelled wrong."

The boy called Raccoon looked at the sign and vaulted over the porch railing, striding across the lawn toward Alden. Ponytail followed. Maybe she'd gone too far. Alden started to reach for her phone but then decided against it. She gripped the handlebars of her bike and planted her feet.

"It's...uh...it's spelled that way to attract more customers," stammered Raccoon.

He was now on the sidewalk next to her bike. Ponytail hovered nearby. One or both of them reeked of something. The smell reminded Alden of dirty socks.

"That's the stupidest thing I've ever heard," she said. "I bet you haven't gotten any business at all."

Raccoon hesitated for a moment and then blurted out, "Uh...not yet. But the sign just went up."

Alden looked at Raccoon with disbelief. The rabid varmint was also an idiot. Despite the cocky tilt to his chin, he wouldn't look at her. His hands were stuffed uncertainly into his pockets.

"It's my uncle's side job. He…uh…*he* wrote the sign." He looked sideways at his friend. "Besides, if I tol' him he'd spelled something wrong, he'd kick my ass. Right, Chris?"

Ponytail Chris guffawed. "Yeah, he would, man!" They high-fived each other.

Alden rolled her eyes and looked back at the sign. "Who drew the picture?"

Raccoon met her eyes this time. "I did," he said, spitting on the ground. "So what?"

Alden looked at the spit next to her sandal with disgust. Raccoon stubbed his shoe at a mound of dirt on the sidewalk and jammed his fists even farther into his pockets.

Alden balanced herself on her bike seat, her toes holding her steady. "Well, it's pretty good." She pushed the pedals and started down the street.

"What's it to ya?" Ponytail yelled after her.

"Shut up, Chris," growled Raccoon.

Alden headed home, pedaling furiously. She couldn't stand kids like Raccoon and Chris. She'd had her share of haters. The guidance counselor in her New York school had tried to teach her coping techniques, but they never worked. Samantha Livingston and Cullen Radcliff had been the worst. The two girls also lived on the Upper West Side, but they spent weekends at their Connecticut homes, playing tennis at the country club and watching Samantha's father play polo. Both girls were skinny, blond, and as perfect as the girls on the cover of their *Teen Vogue* magazines. In class, in the hallway—it didn't matter where—the mean girls' jeers were relentless. Alden despised the cafeteria the most. Cullen would taunt, "Two hamburgers, fries, chocolate pudding, *and* a cookie? Dude, no wonder she's a cow." The other students would immediately tweet their reactions. After that, Alden had always eaten her lunch in the bathroom.

Alden roughly banged through the back door of her kitchen, wiping at her eyes, and cut herself a piece of leftover cake her mom had brought home from a welcoming party at work. As she took a bite, Alden looked down at her plump stomach and thighs pressing against the top and bottom edges of her shorts. Chris and Raccoon's mocking ridicule came back to her, and tears threatened again.

"Screw him," she muttered. The cake tasted good.

Just then, her cell phone vibrated.

"Hi, Cleo. Yeah, I'm home."

"Everything okay?"

"Fine," Alden lied. "I'm going to meet my mom now."

"See you tonight, kid."

Alden grabbed her bike again and started downtown. She rode leisurely through Locust Park across from city hall, admiring the topiary sculptures of lions and giraffes made entirely of plants. Locking her bike in the rack at the public library, she walked past several empty storefronts and stopped in front of the Pantages Theatre. She shielded her eyes from the bright June sunshine and studied the marquee. It looked neglected, unlike the colorful Broadway marquees she was used to.

Alden tugged down her T-shirt and entered the lobby.

"Hello, Alden," greeted Mrs. Waters, the box-office volunteer. "Your mom's still in a meeting with Gina, the board president. She's probably going to be another ten minutes or so."

"Would it be okay if I looked around a little? I haven't seen the theatre yet."

"Go ahead—it's unlocked."

The main theatre doors were glossy black and trimmed with gold. They reminded her of the doors at Radio City Music Hall. She used to go see *The Christmas Spectacular* there with her grandfather every year. Alden pulled on the handle and squeezed her body through the ensuing gap. Center stage, a single lightbulb surrounded by a wire cage on a stand cast irregular shadows on the walls. The theatre was deathly quiet, like a cathedral or a mausoleum, and smelled of dust and mildew. She wrinkled her nose with distaste.

Hundreds of seats spread out in front of her. The proscenium arch over the stage was ornately decorated and adorned with carved stone statues high above the main floor, posed as if watching the audience instead of the action on stage. Elaborate alcoves on either side of the orchestra pit led backstage. Pillars spiraled toward the ceiling, and niches in the walls held gold candelabra. A large balcony rose steeply above the ground floor, extending toward the stage with a horseshoe of theatre boxes.

As she looked more closely, she noticed stuffing bulging through the decaying fabric of the ripped seats and paint peeling from the walls. The theatre looked forgotten and lonely. "What else is new in this town?" Alden thought.

Alden's mom had explained to her that the Pantages was an old vaudeville theatre needing money, renovation, and vision. A local pharmaceutical company was offering a matching grant to help with renovations if her mother could raise $3 million. Pretty daunting. But her mom was determined to bring the theatre and the downtown back to their original glory days. Plus, Alden knew her mom. She'd find a way.

She looked up and sucked in a breath. The enormous domed ceiling was painted like a nighttime sky with three-dimensional fluffy white clouds that stood out on the dark-blue background. Alden imagined she was outside, lying in an open field and staring up at a sky that touched both sides of the earth. At any moment, a shooting star could streak across the painted ceiling.

As Alden gazed upward, a draft of cold air rushed in through the side alcove. Odd…she hadn't heard a door open anywhere. Goose bumps appeared on her bare legs and arms. The lightbulb on the stand flickered and went out. Alden was in complete darkness.

2

Death hath a thousand doors to let out life.

—PHILIP MASSINGER, A VERY WOMAN

Alden's heart rate quickened, and the goose bumps turned to shivers. She groped around in the dark until her hand hit the outside edge of a seat, and she clutched the armrest. She fumbled her way up the aisle, knocking her knees against the hard exterior of the metal seats, her palms damp. She stopped and scolded herself.

"This is stupid! It's probably some kind of power outage."

Alden had managed to get halfway up the aisle, when a noise stopped her. Spinning toward the stage, Alden strained her eyes, willing them to see through the blackness. The cold air was swirling around, enveloping her. She heard it again. A faint, rhythmic tapping and muffled voices. She wanted to run out the main doors, but something kept her in the aisle. Was it fear or curiosity? Then, as suddenly as it had begun, the tapping and voices stopped. The light on the stand flickered back on, and the theatre was once again bathed in shadows.

Alden wrapped her arms around herself, her heart slowing to a normal rate. The theatre looked exactly as it had when she'd first entered. She looked up again at the domed ceiling.

"Pretty amazing, isn't it?"

Alden yelped and then covered her mouth in embarrassment. She turned toward the voice but couldn't see anyone in the dim light.

"Sorry. Didn't mean to scare you."

A slightly disheveled older man walked out of the shadows toward her. He wore khaki pants and loafers, a mustard-colored shirt, and a brown cardigan. The bottom button was missing from his sweater.

8

"The ceiling. It's spectacular."

"Yeah," she replied. "I'm Alden."

"I figured. You're Clare Proctor's daughter."

Alden nodded, surprised. "How did you know?"

"Oh, I know almost everything that goes on around this place." He pointed to the ceiling. "They move, you know, or...*they will move again.*"

"What moves?" asked Alden.

"The clouds. Once the motors are fixed, they actually move across the ceiling. See the white dots up there? The bulbs just need to be replaced, and then they'll twinkle like stars."

Alden gasped. "Wow!" Fascinated, Alden pictured the clouds slowly gliding across the ceiling. "What kind of shows did they have here?"

"Musical comedies, concerts, movies—but back before even *I* was born, there was vaudeville. The Pantages was on the circuit, you know."

Alden had heard of vaudeville but didn't know much about it.

"I'm Walter Douglas. I've been helping around the place." He looked lovingly toward the stage. "This theatre will come back," he said, almost to himself.

"How do you know so much about the clouds and the theatre and stuff? Did you bring your daughter here?"

"And how did you know I had a daughter?" Walter teased as he sat down in the last row of seats.

"Just a guess," Alden said, taking the seat next to him.

"You're right. She loved it here. Lives in Chicago now. In those days, the Pantages was the place to go in Smithfield. You hear a lot of stories about the people who came here—families, teenagers on dates. Couples would look up at that ceiling, watch the clouds and stars...and some," he said, smiling tenderly, "even got engaged before the show." His eyes crinkled the way Grandpa Charlie's used to.

"Really?"

"Me, for one. Row J, seats 101 and 102. I slipped the ring on her finger just before the show started."

"What's your wife's name?"

"Maureen. She died fifteen years ago. Cancer."

"Oh…sorry. My grandpa died in March. Cancer." Tears threatened. Without acknowledging Alden's wet eyes, Walter patted her hand. She blinked them away, folded her legs up on the seat, and changed the subject. "Tell me about vaudeville."

"The shows were a series of acts, kinda like a variety show. There were singers, dancers, magicians, dog acts—something for everyone. The artists performed five or six shows a day. The acts toured the United States, going from theatre to theatre. It was called a circuit. All the greats played the Pantages."

The caged light flickered.

"Mr. Douglas…"

"It's Walter."

"Walter," Alden said, warming to him, "has anything kinda strange happened in this theatre before?"

He caught her eye. "Why do you ask?"

Alden picked at the frayed upholstery on the seat in front of her. "I was in the aisle, and suddenly it got really cold. Then the light went out… and I heard this tapping sound." The ridiculousness of her earlier fear of the darkened theatre embarrassed her now. "It was probably an electricity problem or something…" she mumbled, trailing off.

Before Walter could answer, the main doors of the theatre opened.

"Alden, you in here?"

"Yeah, Mom, over here."

"Hi, Walter. I see you've met Alden."

"Yes, I have. She looks like you, Clare."

Alden scoffed. She had her mom's dark-blond hair and gray eyes but not her tall, willowy figure. "Mom, did you know that the clouds can actually move across the ceiling and that the stars will twinkle once everything's fixed?"

"I have to raise the money first. I need to make the public understand the potential a performing arts center will have for the downtown. Harold Brennan is making it difficult."

"Who's he?"

"A businessman who wants to purchase the Pantages from the city, tear it down, and put in a car dealership."

"Businessman?" Walter snorted. "Crook's a better word."

"Can he buy the theatre?" asked Alden anxiously.

"Not if I can help it," her mom said vehemently. "Besides, the board of directors has a deal with Mayor Klein and the city council. They agreed to hold Brennan off for a year, while I try to turn things around. I filed the paperwork to make the Pantages a historic landmark last week. Once that's approved, no one can tear it down."

Walter turned to Alden and asked, "Alden, how 'bout a backstage tour?"

Alden's stomach lurched with excitement. "Can I, Mom?"

"Sure, honey. But right now, how about some lunch? Walter, would you like to join us?"

"Thanks, but another time. I gotta keep going through those boxes of records. I've barely made a dent."

Walter looked at Alden. "How's Friday?"

"How's tomorrow?" she countered.

Walter chuckled. "Come to the stage door. It's in the alley that runs along the west side of the theatre. I'll leave it unlocked."

Alden took a last look at the ceiling and waved good-bye to Walter, who was dreamily gazing at the stage. Alden and her mom slipped out the main doors, leaving him to his memories.

They walked to Winkie's, one of the few lunch places left downtown. The hostess settled them into a booth and asked for their drink order.

"Water, please," said Alden as she picked up the menu, now regretting chowing down on the cake earlier.

"I'll take an iced tea." Her mom peered at Alden over her menu. "What did you think of the theatre?"

"It's fantastic. I can't wait till the clouds and stars are fixed."

"Alden," she said cautiously, "I'm thinking of starting a theatre camp for students. The ballroom off the balcony lobby is the perfect place to have it. Would you like to be a part of it?"

Apprehensively, Alden asked, "What would the students do in the camp?"

"Singing and dancing lessons, master classes in acting, that sort of thing."

Alden felt a bubble of anticipation. A theatre camp with dance classes! Maybe she could…Alden stopped herself. She couldn't dance—not with her body.

"I don't know…"

"Think about it," her mom pressed.

"Hello, ladies! What'll it be?"

Alden looked up from the menu she'd been staring at to the owner of the voice. One of the man's eyes was focused on Alden, while the other was angled toward the ceiling. She swallowed, trying not to stare.

"It's why everyone calls me Winkie," he said with a grin.

Alden giggled. "I'll have the portobello mushroom sandwich."

"Chicken Caesar for me, Winkie."

"How are things at the Pantages?" Winkie asked.

"Moving along. We're having a fundraising event on Saturday night to kick off our capital campaign."

"Saw it in the paper. You've got my support. 'Bout time something was done with that place. We don't need a used car lot. You know, I'd like to open a bistro in the old guitar factory down the block, but I just can't take the risk until the downtown comes back."

"It's going to, Winkie," Alden's mom said confidently. "When the Pantages reopens, the downtown will be a destination spot."

"Let's hope. Your food'll be out in about ten minutes."

Her mom turned her attention back to Alden. "I got you a new dress for the fundraiser."

"Do I have to go?"

"No, you don't, but I'd like you to. I could use the moral support when I make my big speech."

The last thing Alden wanted to do was sit at a table with people she didn't know. But…it was for her mom and the Pantages, so Alden reluctantly agreed.

"Did you like Walter?"

"He reminded me of Grandpa."

"I thought you might say that."

"He knows a lot about the Pantages."

"Walter was around when the theatre was still in its heyday. It's important to him to save it."

"He asked his wife to marry him at the Pantages."

"Really?"

"Yep," Alden said happily. "Row J, seats 101 and 102."

"No kidding. So what did you do this morning?"

Alden gulped her water. "Um…just rode my bike around."

"See anything interesting?"

"Not really." The happiness Alden had felt sitting with Walter in the Pantages was dampened by the memory of Raccoon's face and his friend Chris. Suddenly she wasn't hungry anymore.

3

I have heard, but not believed, the spirits o' the dead may walk again.

—WILLIAM SHAKESPEARE, THE WINTER'S TALE

The next morning, Alden eagerly got up, showered, dressed, and was in the kitchen before Cleo arrived. Her eyes widened when she saw Alden.

"Hey! You're up early. Hungry?"

"Starving."

"I brought some melon and raspberries for us. They were left over from my culinary class last night."

They went out to the front porch and sat on the steps in the warm June sunshine.

"Geez, get a load of Smithfield's finest," Cleo said, nodding her head toward the street.

Raccoon and Chris were riding their bikes down the block. Alden recognized the cocky tilt of Raccoon's chin and Chris's tight ponytail. Crap. They weren't alone. Bursting out of her low-cut tank top, a girl wearing combat boots and sporting dyed magenta hair tips biked next to them. Multiple piercings in her nose and lip glinted in the bright sunlight.

"I saw those two guys when I was riding around yesterday," Alden whispered to Cleo.

Chris recognized Alden before Raccoon did. "Hey, Jewel, it's the whale we were telling you about—the one who can't ride a bike."

The pierced Jewel taunted, "And look, she's eating!"

"Shut up," snarled Raccoon. Jewel shot him a defensive look but kept her mouth shut. Raccoon's eyes stayed on the sidewalk as he rode past Alden.

Chris yelled over his shoulder, "Stay off Oakdale Street, if you know what's good for ya!" Jewel's laughter faded as they turned the corner.

Alden stared at the untouched bowl of fruit in front of her.

Cleo watched Alden's tight face. "What happened?"

"They said I needed training wheels on my bike and...and...said I was fat." Tears streamed down her cheeks, and she quickly wiped them away.

"You forget about it. You're gonna get as tall as your mom, and your weight will even out, especially if you keep riding your bike. Ignore them, okay?"

"Right, Cleo!" Alden spat out angrily. "That's what adults always tell you to do when someone ridicules you!" She stood up and stomped into the kitchen. She knew she was being immature, but she couldn't help it.

Cleo followed her. "They're morons, Alden."

"Thanks for trying to help, Cleo, but I had worse things happen in New York. I'm used to it." Alden grabbed her cell phone and house keys. "I'll see you later. I'm going to the Pantages."

"Text me when you get there," Cleo called after her. "And if you run into those guys again, I want you to call me, okay?"

"Yeah, yeah, whatever," Alden said as she jerked her bike out of the garage.

Alden tried to force Raccoon, Chris, and Jewel out of her mind as she rode to the theatre. It wasn't easy.

Instead of entering the lobby, she walked past the front of the building and down the alley that ran along the side of the theatre. A fire escape snaked its way down the brick wall and stopped above a door. On it, the words "STAGE DOOR" appeared in faint gold letters.

Opening the door, Alden entered a dim, cool hallway. On her right was a small booth with a half door. A worn bulletin board hung on the wall with CALL-BOARD written above it. The backstage area of the theatre, like the front, suffered from the same neglect.

"I thought I heard someone come in," Walter said, entering the hallway from the stairwell. "Ready?" Alden followed him, practically skipping onto the stage.

"This area," Walter said, gesturing widely around him, "is called the wings. It's where the technicians and actors can stand without the audience seeing them. But you probably already knew that, right?"

"Yeah, my grandpa took me backstage in New York a couple of times." Alden examined a wooden rail running along the side of the wall. Over twenty ropes were looped in figure eights around pegs attached to the rail. Canvas drawstring bags were fastened onto each rope with large metal hooks. "But what's this?"

"It's a counterweight system. Each one of these ropes or lines is strung over a pulley at the top near the ceiling and attached to a baton that runs across the stage."

"What's a baton?" Alden interrupted.

"All those pipes up there. Scenery and lighting hang on the batons. The weight on this side," he said, pointing to the rail, "has to equal the weight hanging on the pipe or baton." Walter looked at Alden to see if she was following.

Alden nodded. She reached up and touched a canvas bag. "What's inside these?"

"Sand. If a backdrop is hung on a baton that weighs, say, a hundred pounds, you'd hang the same amount of sandbags on the rope to balance the load. When the weight is equal, you release the rope from the peg on the rail, and the backdrop flies into place onto the stage."

"Flies?"

"Yes. On a system like this, if the weight is balanced right, the scenery should move effortlessly, just as if it were flying. Of course, most modern theatres have automated systems now."

"How come it's so tall?"

"You have to store the scenery out of sight of the audience when it's not in use. That up there," he said, pointing, "is called a fly loft. Here, I'll show you."

Walter unlashed the rope from the peg at the far end of the rail. He pulled on the rope, and it slid gently through his hands. "I'm flying in the grand curtain, but most stagehands call it the main rag. A faded red curtain slowly lowered from the dark loft above until it touched the stage.

"Sweet," Alden said.

"Anyone can run the flies if they're weighted right. It doesn't take any strength to operate. Wanna try it?" Alden eagerly crossed to the rail.

"Now, since you're flying the main out and back up into the loft, you have to pull the rope on the other side."

Alden put her hands on the rope and pulled. It glided through her hands, and the curtain disappeared into the cavernous ceiling. Walter lashed the rope to the peg and pointed. "Now, go on out there."

Alden walked out onto the stage. The seats were like a sea of red stretching from the main floor up to the balcony. The theatre looked inviting. The lightbulb glowed from inside its wire cage. She forgot the peculiar shadows the light had cast before—now, they danced.

"It's a totally different perspective standing here and looking out, isn't it?" Walter mused.

"What kind of light is this?"

"A ghost light. At the end of a show, the last person to leave the theatre has to turn it on. It stays on until the next performance."

"Why's it called a ghost light?"

"Well, that question has a two-part answer." Walter sat on the edge of the stage, his legs dangling into the pit. Alden joined him. "It's the light left on so ghosts won't inhabit the theatre. But I like the more intriguing explanation. It's tied to the legend of how the light got its name."

"What legend?"

"The legend of the ghost light. The light left on *for* the theatre ghosts."

"*Theatre ghosts*? No one really believes there are ghosts in theatres, do they?"

"Some people do. There've been ghost sightings in theatres for hundreds of years. Some theatres have one that haunts the place, and other theatres have multiple ghosts. Usually it's only the people who work in the theatre who see and hear them."

"Who are these ghosts supposed to have been?"

"Actors, directors, magicians, even stagehands—anyone with a connection to the theatre. They die and haunt a place because their souls can't move on. Some people believe that theatre ghosts are only semidead, because they're tied to a particular theatre and can't leave. In the legend, theatre ghosts are earthbound, stuck in the theatre forever."

"But why would ghosts need a light after everyone's left the theatre?"

"It's the light that theatre ghosts use for their performances."

"They put on a ghost show when no one's around?" Alden blurted out too loudly.

"Apparently."

Alden looked out into the empty Pantages. She remembered the sudden blast of cold air and the ghost light flickering and going out. Lowering her voice, she asked, "Walter, does every theatre use one of these ghost lights?"

"Most do."

"But the other stuff—that's only a superstition, right?"

"Yes...and no."

Alden's teeth began to chatter.

"Legends have to come from somewhere."

"Do you think the Pantages has a ghost?" Alden asked. But she knew the answer before Walter spoke.

"I do. Actually, I think it has several."

4

Curtain! Fast music! Light! Ready for the last finale! Great!
The show looks good, the show looks good!

—FLORENZ ZIEGFELD JR.

"The Pantages is haunted?" Alden stared at the ghost light. "How do you know? Have you…have you seen any ghosts?"

"Not exactly, but there've been signs." Walter stood up and held out his hand to Alden. "Come on, let's finish our tour. Ever been on a catwalk?"

Alden wanted to hear more about the Pantages ghosts, but right now she was too timid to ask him. *Ghosts!* Was it possible? Maybe Walter was just teasing her. She followed Walter up a spiral staircase that wound up into the fly loft, her sandals clanging on the metal steps. They climbed several stories until they reached the top, near the roof of the theatre. The staircase connected to an iron walkway that extended across the stage, high above the wooden floor. Panting, Alden stopped at the top to catch her breath.

"Catwalks get their name because cats can balance themselves on things that are narrow and high. Up here, stagehands have easy access to the lighting and hanging scenery."

Walter nimbly walked across the catwalk as Alden tentatively followed, gripping the railing tightly, feeling slightly light-headed. Trying to forget her fear of heights, she looked down at the stage and imagined performers entertaining audiences far below. Was it possible that ghosts performed here too? If the Pantages did have ghosts, what did they look like? How could they have died and still continue to live as half-dead spirits? How would they feel about her mom reopening the theatre?

Walter had reached the other side of the catwalk. At the end was a metal door with a large bolt lock. He slid it over and opened the door. Bright sunlight poured into the theatre.

"This is the emergency exit for stagehands in case of a fire. It leads to the alley that runs along the side of the theatre." With the sunlight streaming through the fire-escape door and into the theatre, it was hard to imagine there could be ghosts floating around. "Would you like to see where I've been working?"

Alden nodded, realizing she hadn't asked Walter what his job was.

They retraced their steps and entered a room behind the wings. Boxes were everywhere, on desks and shelves, piled on wooden filing cabinets. Dozens of picture frames were stacked haphazardly against the cabinets. On one side of the room was a plastic folding table with neat piles of pamphlets and papers on it. The table was the only bit of organization in the room.

"I call it the archive room. It was probably the management's office at one time. In here," he said, waving his hand around the room, "is the history of the Pantages Theatre."

Alden picked up a pamphlet from the table and opened it.

PANTAGES THEATRE BILL
1918

Inside was a list of acts. "Is this a playbill from one of the shows?" she asked.

"That's right, and in these boxes are pictures, contracts, newspaper reviews, invoices—anything necessary for running a theatre on the vaudeville circuit. My job's been to organize all this stuff. Your mom wants to turn the lobby into a small museum, where the history of the Pantages will be displayed."

"Walter, how do you know so much about vaudeville?"

"My grandparents were hoofers and performers on the vaudeville circuit. They traveled by train from theatre to theatre. They played the Pantages."

Alden could hardly believe it. Walter's grandparents had actually performed at this theatre!

"But then, it was over."

"Why? What happened?"

"Vaudeville died. Talking pictures became the rage, and Hollywood became glamorous. Vaudeville slowly disappeared."

"What did your grandparents do then?"

"They moved to California, like everyone else in the business. Luckily, they got long-term contracts at one of the movie studios. My parents were a screenwriting team. I grew up in California. Eventually, I came to Smithfield University to teach." Walter picked up one of the pictures from the table. "I enjoyed teaching film history, but there's something about vaudeville..." His voice drifted off.

"What's a hoofer?"

Walter laughed, his smile crooked with memories. "Vaudeville lingo. Hoofers are dancers—primarily tap dancers. Vaudeville had lots of them, like Peg Leg Bates, Bill Robinson, and the Nicholas Brothers. Hey, how 'bout a little help?"

"Sure," Alden said, nodding.

"Grab that box over there. Separate the programs from the pictures and anything that looks like order forms or invoices. I've organized piles of each on this table."

Alden picked up the box Walter had pointed to and quickly set to work, feeling as if she was digging for buried treasure. "What other vaudeville *lingo* is there?" she asked Walter.

"A headliner was the entertainer, who was the star—the person who could bring in the crowds. The bill was the list of acts, and comedians were the bananas."

Alden laughed. "Comedians were called bananas?"

"And the most *popular* comedian was called the top banana. Comedians would do a routine about bananas, and then they'd slip on the peel and fall on their rear ends." She laughed even harder picturing it.

Alden spent the next couple of hours learning about slapstick comedy, baggy-pants comedians, and showgirls.

"Well, look at this," Walter said as he pulled a black-and-white photo out of a box. Alden peered over his shoulder. The girl appeared to be in her early twenties with dark hair and huge eyes, a flirtatious look on her pouty face. She was wearing a short, beaded gown. In her hand she held an enormous fan made of feathers. The caption read, "Olive Thomas, Ziegfeld Girl."

"What's with the fan?"

"To dance with. Ziegfeld girls were known for their beauty and their extravagant but skimpy costumes. Ziegfeld, who produced the *Follies*, liked to tease his audiences and have the girls cover up with props like fans or scarves. This one," Walter continued, "was rumored to be Ziegfeld's mistress. They say her ghost haunts the New Amsterdam Theatre on Forty-Second Street."

Alden looked squarely at Walter. "You said earlier that the Pantages might have a ghost."

"Did I?" he said evasively. Walter looked at her eager face and said softly, "It's just a feeling; I could be out of my mind..." Clumsily, he gathered some papers from the table and stuffed them into a file. "I'm an old man, Alden."

"I wanna know."

"Well, it's just a hunch, you understand." Alden nodded, holding her breath, willing him to go on. "Last April, when I first started coming to the theatre, I heard voices, but I couldn't find anyone in the building."

"Go on."

"And then there was a strange green light moving around the theatre..." Walter trailed off and glanced quickly at Alden. "You must think I'm crazy. I've never mentioned any of this to your mother..."

"What else did you see?"

"I...I saw what looked like a man sitting in one of the theatre boxes." Walter quickly moved to the other side of the room and jammed the file into the cabinet, evading Alden's eyes. "I chalked it up to the feeble mind of a senior citizen."

"There's more...isn't there?"

Walter sighed. "Yes. I found a fascinating newspaper review about the Gleason sisters. They were regulars on the vaudeville circuit. The first time they played the Pantages, the local critic couldn't get enough of them. He raved about their talent and charisma."

"What was their act?" asked Alden.

"Juggling. They juggled everything from plates to flaming torches. While I was reading the article, I heard talking on the stage. I left the clipping on this table and searched the whole theatre, but I couldn't find anyone. I felt ridiculous, as if I'd imagined the whole thing. When I came back to the archive room, the article was gone."

"What do you think happened to it?" asked Alden anxiously.

Walter shook his head as if trying to shake away the memory. "Who knows? Probably the forgetfulness of the elderly."

Walter pulled on his brown cardigan. "I've got to stop for today. I have an alumni meeting at the university."

Sorry their morning together was over, Alden followed him to the stage door. Walter locked it behind them, and they walked down the alley into the bright sunshine.

"Walter, where did the Gleason sisters go after playing the Pantages?"

"They never performed their act again. The day after they opened at the Pantages, they were found dead in their dressing room."

5

No one is useless in this world who lightens the burdens of another.

—C*HARLES* D*ICKENS*

Over the next few weeks, Alden rode her bike downtown and spent almost every day with Walter, working in the archive room. Thankfully, she hadn't seen Raccoon or Chris again. The fundraiser party for the Pantages had been a financial success—and, luckily, hadn't been as painful as Alden had feared. She'd sat at a table with Walter and a couple who owned WZBS, the local television station. She'd also met Meghan and Jenna Friedman, twins who would be in Alden's grade in school in the fall. Meghan and Jenna's parents were big supporters of the renovation of the Pantages because their daughters loved the theatre. The twins had invited Alden to come over and swim in their pool the next day.

Alden proudly remembered her mom's pitch for money to save the theatre.

"The Pantages is a local treasure, a jewel in the heart of this community. But it's more than that. This theatre is the future—our future together. I came to Smithfield with my daughter, Alden, because I believe in this project. After World War I, the first buildings in Europe to be *rebuilt* weren't the government offices or the stores. They were the theatres. There the citizens gathered for a brief escape from their war-torn world. During the Great Depression, Americans spent their few pennies going to plays and movies. Today, we still need to share experiences together—and what better way than in a theatre? The Pantages needs to be rebuilt and reopened so that *we*, the citizens of Smithfield, can gather to enjoy and experience the arts collectively and communally together."

When Alden's mom had finished, loud, raucous applause had broken out, and guests had jumped to their feet, cheering. Walter had started to chant, "Save the Pantages! Save the Pantages!" Swept up by her mother's words, Alden had joined him, chanting, "Save the Pantages!" Soon, everyone had picked up the chant. "Save the Pantages!"

The theatre camp for students had started. Alden's mom continued to press her to join. "The students are nice theatre kids. Some are your age." Pulling down her blouse over her middle, Alden ignored her.

Since her first day working with Walter, Alden had tried to get more information out of him about the death of the Gleason sisters, but he'd been pretty closemouthed, answering her probing questions with vague answers. The only thing he'd told her was that the police had suspected foul play.

"Anyone with a connection to the theatre could be a theatre ghost," Walter had said. Was it just a coincidence? Could the Gleason sisters be the ghosts of the Pantages?

Alden showered quickly and pulled on her shorts. They weren't as hard to button over her stomach now and felt looser around her hips. She had been so busy working in the archive room that she had forgotten her usual craving for snacks.

Alden grabbed her bike and rode to the Pantages. Instead of using the stage door, she entered through the lobby, ran up the stairs, and peeked into her mom's office. Seeing her daughter, she put down her phone, her face flushed. Alden plopped into the chair opposite her desk.

"Do you remember meeting Greg Carter at the fundraiser party?" her mom asked.

"Isn't he a bigwig with the company that's helping to raise money for the Pantages?"

"Yes. Whatever money we raise will be matched by the Glenco Corporation." Rushing on, her mother stated, "He asked me out to dinner." She searched Alden's face anxiously.

"And?" asked Alden.

"Well, is it okay?"

"Mom, I'm not gonna try to get you and Dad back together like some *Parent Trap* plot, if that's what you're thinking. Do you like him?"

"I…yes."

"Then go out with him!" Alden jumped up. "I'm going to the archive room. I'll see you when you get home. Not too late, now!" Alden teased.

Her mom's bright face lightened Alden's mood. Her mom and dad had divorced several years ago. Alden figured that a lot of her parents' problems had stemmed from the fact that her father had never been around. He was an independent film director and had spent months at a time away. She'd quickly gotten used to both his prolonged absences and the divorce. It had taken her mom a lot longer.

The night before they'd left for Michigan, Alden's dad had taken her out to dinner. Alden had inhaled the burritos and rice enthusiastically, but her dad embarrassed her. He had talked loudly on his cell as restaurant patrons shot them disapproving looks. Her father was oblivious.

"Dad!" she had hissed, pointing at his phone.

He'd put his hand up and said, "In a minute, Alden."

She'd slid down in her chair. Finally he hung up and asked for the check.

Walking home with him, Alden had said softly, "You missed Grandpa's funeral." Actually, she was glad he hadn't been there. It would have humiliated her if he had tried to direct her grandfather's funeral as if it were a movie script. The grief had been hard enough.

"Yeah…how was it?"

"Pretty rough," she said, blinking back tears. "I miss him."

His phone had rung, and he'd taken the call.

Later, as she lay in bed, she'd heard fragments of her parents' living-room conversation.

"You know our agreement says you can't move more than a hundred miles from New York City!"

Alden hadn't been able to hear her mother's reply.

"I'll take you back to court, Clare! I need to see my daughter."

Their voices had gotten louder then, and Alden didn't have to strain to hear anymore.

"You haven't seen her in five months, Joe!" her mother replied. Alden could hear the edge in her voice.

"I was on location!" he spat out.

"And now you're back for what…a couple of days? You take her out to dinner, ease your guilt, and then you won't see her again for months." This time, her mother's voice was flat, resigned. "It should hardly matter where Alden and I live."

"Your brother encouraged you to take this job. He never liked me."

"Keller had nothing to do with my decision."

Alden's Uncle Keller was an actor, who lived on the West Coast. She knew he missed them, but her uncle's aversion to his brother-in-law had resulted in few visits but a lot of FaceTime. She'd turned over and pulled her comforter closer to her chin. Her dad wasn't very good at this, and her mom was tough. Truth was, Alden didn't care how much she saw her dad.

"You can't buy affection, Joe. I'm taking this job in Michigan. Don't turn this into another battle just so you can pretend you're a good father. It's a great opportunity for me, and it'll be good for Alden. She misses my dad. It's been hard on her. Maybe…maybe she'll make some friends in Michigan. She certainly doesn't have any here."

"Ouch," Alden had thought. So her mom had noticed.

Her dad's cell phone had rung then. Alden assumed he'd taken the call when she heard the apartment door open and close. Her mother had won. The next day, they'd left for Smithfield.

Running down the stairs from her mother's office, Alden stopped awkwardly, quickly forgetting her parents. Camp students were gathered in small groups in the lobby, some talking, some texting, and some listening to music.

Three girls were seated on the floor, singing snatches of music from a Broadway songbook. "I love that song! Let's sing it again," the girls squealed and started over.

On the staircase leading up to the balcony, a pretty, curvy girl with dark hair and green eyes stood surrounded by a group of admiring students.

"I just got cast in the Smithfield Mall television spot."

"Morgan, when are you going to New York City?"

"End of the summer. I'll be interviewing with some agents."

"Will you see a Broadway show?"

"Heeeyeah!" Morgan scoffed.

Alden bravely joined the group on the stairs. "I just moved here from New York," she said.

"Did you have an agent?" Morgan asked coolly.

"Well, no, I'm not an actress, I—"

"Come on, it's time for class," Morgan interrupted. The camp students grabbed their dance bags and started up the stairs.

Alden numbly walked backstage, stung by Morgan's rudeness. "I'd rather spend my time helping Walter anyway," she thought.

Alden looked around the archive room. They'd made progress. Files were now in the proper order and clearly labeled. The old office now had a feeling of organization instead of its original chaos. Alden smiled to herself, proud that she had been a part of the improvement. Alden and Walter shared stories while they worked—Walter of his growing up in Hollywood and Alden with accounts of going to Broadway shows with Grandpa Charlie.

Alden scolded herself, saying, "I'm daydreaming, and there's still so much to do!" She picked up a box she'd been wanting to tackle and opened the cardboard folds.

TAP...tap...tap...tap, tap, tap, **TAP**, tap, tap. Alden looked toward the door. **TAP**...tap...tap...tap, tap, tap, **TAP**, tap, tap. It was the same rhythmic sound she'd heard her first day in the theatre when the ghost light had suddenly gone out. The sound was coming from the stage!

Quietly she crept down the hall and then stopped in the doorway, listening. The tapping continued, strong and loud. Slowly she tiptoed into the wings, running her tongue around her dry mouth. The tapping stopped, and Alden froze. She held her breath, waiting. If the Pantages had a ghost, would it want to be discovered? She breathed out slowly, clenching and unclenching her fists. Would they harm her for intruding? She thought about returning to the archive room, but then the tapping began again.

Her knees trembling, Alden moved between the curtains and peeked onto the stage. What she saw disappointed her. It wasn't a ghost. It was a girl! She was around Alden's age with long blond hair pulled back and tied with a wide ribbon. She wore a simple dress with a round collar, and she was dancing. Her brow was creased with concentration.

TAP…tap…tap…tap, tap, tap, **TAP**, tap, tap.

This girl practiced her tap dancing on the stage! Alden felt stupid. Hoping for a ghost, she'd imagined a white, misty creature floating over the stage—a transparent shape, strange and ethereal. What an idiot! Alden had allowed herself to get caught up in the ghost light legend, a ridiculous fantasy.

She turned her attention back to the girl and watched her dance. She repeated her tap rhythms over and over. Occasionally she stopped and spat out, "No!" Then she would start again. She was actually pretty good. Alden loved tap-dancing movies and recognized the time step she was beating out on the floor. It dawned on Alden that this girl was probably someone from the theatre camp, who'd snuck down from the balcony ballroom to dance on the stage!

Boldly, Alden walked out of the wings.

"Hi."

The girl abruptly stopped dancing and turned toward her. "Oh, hi. I'm practicing. I know I shouldn't be here; it's just that I love looking out and pretending there's an audience out there. I wanna be a professional." She scuffed her shoe and did a quick tapping spin.

"I'm Alden." She waited for the girl to share her name, but she just continued tapping in a bigger circle. "My mom's the director of development for the Pantages."

The girl stopped and looked at Alden nervously. "Please don't tell her I've been using the stage! I don't wanna get into trouble. I'm not hurting anything."

"I won't."

She tapped over to where Alden stood. "I'm sorry. I'm being rude." She formally held out her hand. "Juliette Stanton." Alden shook her hand. "Gloria and Grace call me Juliette, but you can call me Julie."

"Who are Gloria and Grace?" Alden asked.

"My aunts. I live with them." She smiled at Alden and executed another tap move. "That's a pullback. Do you tap dance?"

"No." Alden cocked her head, watching Julie dance. "How long have you been dancing?"

"As long as I can remember. I think my mother started me when I was two."

Julie didn't say anything more about her mom, and Alden decided it wasn't polite to ask why she lived with her aunts. Instead, she asked shyly, "Would you like to see the archive room?"

"What's that?"

"An office that's backstage. I've been going through old documents and organizing them. Come on!" Alden led her through the wings and into the backstage hallway, Julie's shoes tapping on the wooden floor in the wings and then on the concrete hallway.

"There's all kinds of stuff in here from when the Pantages used to be a theatre."

"It still *is* a theatre," declared Julie fiercely.

Alden tugged on her shirt. "I...I meant...a *working* theatre." Alden grabbed a stack of programs, eager to please her. "See these playbills? They list the acts that played the Pantages during vaudeville!"

Julie glanced uneasily toward the hallway. She seemed to have little interest in the archives that Alden had found so inspiring. She had hoped Julie would find the history of the Pantages as absorbing as she herself did. Self-doubt and insecurity welled up in her. Typical. Just like everyone else, Julie too thought she was weird.

"Is it really okay to be in here?" Julie asked.

Alden smiled encouragingly at her. "Yeah. You can use the stage. My mom won't mind. She's cool." Alden perched on the desk. "I've been working with Walter. My mom asked him to go through all this stuff."

"Is he the old man who's always around?"

"Yeah." Did Julie know Walter?

"He tap dances, you know."

"What? Walter taps?" Alden was astonished. "I...I had no idea. You've seen him dance?"

"Sometimes, at the end of the day when I'm waiting for my aunts, I sneak into the back of the theatre and watch him. He practices on the stage, just like I do."

Walter's grandparents had been hoofers. Maybe it was possible.

"I have this idea..." Julie faltered and then continued hesitantly. "Lessons. I'd love some lessons. Do you think Walter would teach me?" She rushed on. "He's one of the best tappers I've ever seen, and I'm having trouble with the double pullback, plus I can't seem to get my triple-time step as clean as it should be."

"Sure, I can ask him." She wondered how Walter would react to his secret having been discovered by an ambitious theatre-camp student.

"Gosh, Alden, thanks." Julie tapped over to the desk and hugged Alden. "If I could work with him, I'd be so grateful! I know he could help me improve." Julie's hug and innocent display of gratitude caught Alden off guard. She was unable to respond. Julie released her and tapped happily to the doorway. "Well, I better get back upstairs before they miss me. See ya."

Julie breezed out of the room, down the hall, and across the stage, tapping the whole way. With her exit, Alden felt strangely empty. She hoped she'd see Juliette Stanton again.

Uninspired to continue her archive work for the day, Alden turned the interior lock on the stage door and shut it behind her. Retrieving her bike at the library, she thoughtfully rode through Locust Park, trying to comprehend the fact that Walter was a secret tap dancer. The sound of another bike coming up behind her jolted her out of her daydream. Alden glanced behind her. It was Raccoon.

6

Courage is resistance to fear, mastery of fear, not absence of fear.

—MARK TWAIN

"Wait up!" he yelled.

Alden pedaled harder.

"Really...wait up. Can I talk to you?" He'd caught up with her. She gave him a withering look.

"Look," he said breathlessly, "I'm sorry about that first day I met you. I know I was mean."

Alden stopped her bike, balancing herself. She stared at him, defenses ready. Raccoon's eyes were a piercing blue, like beach glass against his deeply tanned face, his brown wavy hair curling just above his shoulders. Today he wore a regular T-shirt. "Guess he realized he didn't have any muscles," Alden thought gloatingly.

Aloud, she warily asked, "Whaddya want?"

Raccoon walked his bike over to a tree at the edge of the park and leaned it against the trunk. He pulled a pad out of his back pocket.

"You said something that day...about the sign." He scuffed his dirty shoe on the grass.

"Yeah, that your uncle can't spell."

"No...not the spelling part." He was obviously uncomfortable. Alden didn't try to put him at ease.

"Here." He thrust the notepad toward her.

Alden looked at his outstretched hand and then at his face. The cocky tilt to his chin was gone, and his eyes were hopeful. He waited, watching her. Alden pushed down her kickstand and took the notepad from him.

"What's this?"

Raccoon didn't answer and thrust his hands into his pockets.

Alden opened it. On the first page was a drawing of the man with the eagle tattoo, identical to the sign at Raccoon's house on Oakdale Street. She flipped to the next page. It was a sketch of a willow tree, its branches hanging over a pond, a bird perched on the bank. Near the water was a small child skipping a stone. Fascinated, Alden turned to the next picture—a rusty, broken-down truck in a field. Alden looked up from the notepad.

"These are pretty good."

Raccoon scuffed his feet, remaining silent. Alden turned the page. There was a picture of a squirrel scurrying up a tree. She recognized the fountain and band shell in the background as Locust Park. "You drew these?"

Raccoon nodded. Alden handed him back the notepad. He stuffed it back into his pocket, sat down, and started pulling clumps of grass up with his fists. Guardedly, she sat down next to him.

"What do you do at that place every day?" he asked.

"What?"

"You know…that building near the library."

"The Pantages? How did you—"

"I've seen you. What's down that alley?"

"You've been following me?"

"I was curious," Raccoon answered.

"The stage door."

He frowned, looking confused. She repeated, "The stage door. The Pantages is an old theatre. It's a back entrance. My mom works there, and I'm helping this guy with…"

Alden stopped. Why was she telling him this? He and his jerk-off friend had made her miserable. She jumped up and walked over to her bike. Annoyed with herself, she said, "Why do you care where I go?"

"I wanted to show you my drawings to…to see what you thought. I wanted your opinion because you'd said the sign was pretty good…but every time I tried to talk to you, I…chickened out."

Alden softened. "Do you wanna be an artist?"

"I think so, but my uncle...he wouldn't get it."

"Your friend Chris—"

"Sucks," he interrupted.

Alden threw her leg over her bike seat. "I like your drawings. I think they're grand." She watched as Raccoon's eyes twitched, a smile tugging at his lip. "I mean, they're...cool."

Raccoon got on his bike and rode next to her. At the corner of Duke and Main, Alden said, "I didn't like you at first. I'm not sure I like you now."

"I know. I was a jerk." Raccoon's eyes met hers, his chin level, no hint of its customary upward slant. "I'm sorry."

"I'm Alden."

Raccoon nodded and then continued down Main Street, presumably on his way to his uncle's house. Alden watched him for a brief minute and then started home, detouring toward Grover Place. She never would have guessed the guy she'd detested a month ago was the artistic type. Maybe Raccoon wasn't as tough as he liked to pretend. Even so, Alden wasn't ready to trust him—yet.

"Stop right there, fat girl."

Startled, she didn't watch where she was going and crashed into a fire hydrant.

"Ow!" She looked down. Her front tire was now out of line with the handlebars. "Great."

Chris and Jewel sat under a couple of trees at the end of the street, laughing and smoking a joint.

"You still need those training wheels," mocked Chris as he handed the joint to Jewel and got on his bike. "I'm gettin' sick of seeing your fat face."

Alden started walking her bike in the other direction. She could feel her cell phone in her pocket—maybe this time she should call Cleo.

Jewel jumped on the bike seat behind Chris. Alden broke into a jog still pushing her bike.

"Hey, I'm talking to you!" Chris's voice was demanding.

Alden ignored him. Her front tire was flat. She pushed her bike harder, but Chris and Jewel were even with her in seconds.

"Stay away from here. This is where we hang, and we don't wanna see your sorry ass."

First Oakdale Street and now Grover Place? Did they think they owned the whole neighborhood? Alden was panting from the exertion of running and pushing her bike. She could smell the weed on their clothes and breath. Then she saw what she needed lying in the road. Alden glanced quickly over at them. They were stoned, their bike wobbling back and forth. She pushed her legs and body as hard as she could and managed to get a few paces ahead of them. Alden reached down, grabbed the tree branch, and stuck it through the spokes of Chris's bike.

Metal clanged. Chris and Jewel shrieked. Bodies and bike hit the pavement.

"You bitch!"

Alden looked over her shoulder. Jewel lay next to the curb, with Chris heaped under the bike in the middle of the road. Alden took off.

7

*When you do dance, I wish you a wave o' the sea
that you might ever do nothing but that.*

—WILLIAM SHAKESPEARE, THE WINTER'S TALE

Every day since he'd shown her his drawings, Raccoon caught up with Alden on her way to the theatre, and they would ride downtown together. They talked about Smithfield, New York City, a little about Raccoon's art, but very little about his home life. Chris and Jewel never came up, but she assumed he'd heard about what had happened. When they arrived at the stage door, Alden would ask Raccoon to come in and meet Walter, but he always refused.

Inside the archive room, Alden worked harder than ever. Now that Julie had revealed Walter's secret, she had begged him to dance for her.

"Julie says you're one of the best tap dancers she's ever seen."

"I'm rusty, Alden," he'd said, declining.

Then one hot day, as they were sorting a box of contracts in the archive room, Alden heard the familiar tapping on the stage.

TAP...tap...tap...tap, tap, tap, **TAP**, tap, tap.

"It's her!" she said, grabbing Walter's hand and leading him into the cool wings. But the stage was empty. "Julie? I thought I heard her out here," she said, disappointed.

Walter looked around curiously and then executed a brief tap routine.

"Hey, you're terrific!" said Alden. He really *could* tap dance! Walter continued with an intricate series of taps.

"Hi, Alden."

Startled, Alden turned around. "Oh, there you are!"

Julie was anxiously watching Walter, waiting for Alden to introduce them.

"Juliette Stanton, this is my friend Walter Douglas. His grandparents were hoofers in vaudeville."

"Mr. Douglas, I've watched you practice from the back of the house. I'm sorry I was spying on you, but I just couldn't help it. You're fantastic!"

"Thank you," Walter replied humbly. "And it's Walter."

Julie gulped and blurted out, "Would you teach me? My aunts said I could, if it's all right with you. I love tap dancing, and I wanna improve. I promise I'll work really hard."

Walter studied Juliette. Alden crossed her fingers. She wanted him to say yes. Julie wanted it so badly!

"I'm not sure there are any new tricks you can learn from an old guy like me, but we'll give it a try—on one condition. Alden has to join us and learn to tap dance as well."

"Me? No, I..."

"I know how much you love musicals, Alden. You'll like dancing," coaxed Walter.

"Please, Alden?" Julie begged.

Alden desperately looked at both of them. "Would it just be us? None of the other camp kids?"

"Just us for the time being." Walter said. "Maybe after you learn a little and get your confidence up, you can join the theatre camp, as your mom has been itching for you to do."

Secretly she had dreamed of dancing. But every attempt her mother had made to enroll her in a dance class, Alden had refused. But maybe now, with just Walter and Julie...

"Okay," she said, timidly agreeing.

Julie smiled brilliantly and bounced up and down on her toes.

A few days later, Julie presented Alden with a pair of tap shoes. "I hope they fit."

Alden looked at the gift in her hands. They were old, scuffed in several places, and the toe of the right foot had a hole in the leather. "They used to be my Aunt's when she was little. I know they're pretty beat up, but at least we can get started with these until your mom gets you your own pair."

"Thanks." Alden recalled her mother's expression when she shyly told her she wanted to study tap dancing with Walter. Her mother was surprised, but she offered to get her tap shoes as soon as possible.

"Come on, let's start with some basics until Walter gets here."

For the next hour, Julie took Alden through shuffles and ball changes and the trick of shifting your weight back and forth from leg to leg. Alden struggled awkwardly but by the time Walter arrived, she was able to execute flaps across the stage.

"See, you're a natural," said Julie.

The lessons began. At the end of the day, when the other theatre-camp participants were heading out the lobby doors to the street, Julie would enter the theatre through the black-and-gold doors and join Alden and Walter on the stage for tap dancing. Walter began with basic steps for Alden and more advanced ones for Julie. Alden felt like she had two left feet—no, three left feet. Walter and Julie made it look so easy. They drilled step after step, tirelessly. Walter was in great shape for a man his age. Alden, on the other hand, would leave the theatre with her T-shirt soaked with sweat, her muscles quivering.

They soon settled into a comfortable routine together. Alden and Walter were close to finishing the organization of the archive room. They had collected plenty of materials for her mother to display in the lobby, and several afternoons a week, tap-dancing lessons took place on the stage. Alden had picked up tap terminology—shuffle, ball change, shim-sham, and now she knew what a pullback was. Her tap dancing was improving. She suspected that Walter enjoyed the dance lessons as much as she and Julie did. For Alden, it was a fantastic time. She couldn't wait to get to the theatre every day. Summers in New York, she had always spent by herself. Summer at the Pantages, though, was the best time she'd ever had.

One late August afternoon, Alden rode to the theatre and ran up to her mom's office.

"Hi," she greeted Gina, the theatre board president.

"Hey, you look different."

"Thanks," Alden said self-consciously but pleased. "New haircut."

"It looks great."

"Is my mom busy?"

"No, she's just finishing up for the day. Go on in."

Alden pushed open her mom's office door. Clare looked up from a letter she was reading, her face shining.

"Alden! What's up?"

"I just stopped in to say hi. I like my new haircut. Thanks for taking me to your new salon this morning."

"I'm glad. Allie, I have incredible news! Because we've done so well with donations and camp enrollment, Glenco is going to release the first million dollars of the matching grant to us ahead of schedule. Greg and I are going to discuss the upcoming renovations over dinner."

"Another date? You've been seeing a lot of each other lately," Alden teased.

"Stop," said Claire, gently shoving Alden.

"Have a good time, Mom. I'm gonna go say hi to Walter and Julie. I'll see you at home."

"From your description of her, I can't seem to place Julie as a theatre-camp student. I'd come say hello now, but I'm supposed to meet Greg at the restaurant, and I'm already late."

"She's a great hoofer."

"I'd love to see her dance. Tell her I'm anxious to meet her. See ya later tonight." She kissed Alden and left the office.

Alden crossed through the lobby, entered the theatre, and ran down the aisle. Julie was sitting on the edge of the stage, removing her tap shoes.

"Hey, my mom wants to meet you. I told her what a great dancer you are."

"I...I can't today." Julie grabbed her tap shoes, jamming them into her dance bag, and said distractedly, "Walter's already left, and...well... my aunts are waiting."

"Oh. Okay," said Alden, disappointed that Julie didn't want to hang out a little. "I guess I'll see you tomorrow."

"Sure. See ya." Julie shouldered her bag and ran up the aisle. Alden watched her hasty exit. Julie seemed in an unusual hurry. Puzzled, Alden crossed through the wings and into the archive room. She grabbed a stack of photographs and began sorting them. Before she knew it, it was past dinnertime.

Reluctantly, Alden grabbed her stuff. She turned the latch on the inside of the stage door, stepped into the alley, and checked to make sure the door was locked. Lost in thought, she skipped down the alley. The summer in Smithfield had gone by fast. New York was becoming a fading memory. Alden was actually looking forward to attending her new school. She was entering the ninth grade at the junior high in her neighborhood. She wondered if Julie or Raccoon attended the same school and reminded herself to ask them.

Alden reached the end of the alley, turned toward the library, and then stopped abruptly. Standing on the curb in front of the Pantages were Chris and Jewel. Chris had pulled the front of his T-shirt over his head and gathered it behind his neck. Tattooed on his chest was a picture of a snake wrapped around a pistol. Jewel wore her usual black combat boots.

What should she do? If she walked calmly by them, maybe they would just insult her and let her pass unscathed. The theatre was closed, so there was no chance of escaping through the lobby doors, and she'd just locked the stage door.

"I have no choice," she thought nervously. She had to walk past them to get her bike. Alden started down the sidewalk.

"There she is! I told you she hung out around this place." Chris started menacingly toward her, and Jewel was close behind.

Alden's throat tightened, and she couldn't swallow. Fumbling, she reached for her cell phone but realized with horror that it wasn't in her pocket. She always had it with her! She'd been in such a rush this morning to get to her haircut appointment that she'd forgotten it. Shame overcame her. Automatic dial to Cleo didn't help when her cell was in her bedroom.

"We want a little payback after that stunt you pulled," threatened Jewel, now within twenty feet of where Alden stood.

They broke into a trot, and blindly Alden took off down the alley. Instinctively she had turned toward the Pantages, thinking foolishly that somehow the theatre would protect her. Choosing the alley had been stupid, though—it was a dead end. Now what was she going to do?

With her heart thudding, Alden looked for something she could use as a weapon, hoping another large stick would miraculously appear. She glanced up. The fire escape! If she could reach up and pull the ladder section down, she could climb up and get away from them. It was her only hope.

Alden sprinted toward it. She jumped, trying to grasp the bottom of the metal ladder, and missed. Irritated with herself, she leaped again, stretching both her hands toward the bottom rung.

"Oh no, you don't." Chris grabbed the back of her shirt and pulled. She lost her balance momentarily, righted herself, and jerked away from him. Her T-shirt tore as Chris lost his grip. Alden staggered away from him and turned to run toward the street, but Jewel was blocking her way. Using both hands, Jewel pushed Alden's shoulders and slammed her into the alley's brick wall. Searing pain shot through her back, and her eyes stung with tears.

"How's that feel?" yelled Jewel angrily, spittle shooting out of her lips. Her eyes were bloodshot.

Chris moved next to Alden and growled at her with marijuana breath. "This'll teach you to mess with us."

Jewel pinned her against the wall, the bricks scraping Alden's shoulders through her torn shirt. She pushed her face into Alden's. "Hey! I sprained my wrist because of you! And what's going on with Raccoon? I know he's been coming around this place lookin' for you."

Alden gasped out, "Nothing. We've just talked a little." She guessed Jewel didn't know anything about Raccoon's notebook of sketches. She struggled to escape but couldn't break away from Jewel's grip. Jewel kicked Alden's shin with her combat boot.

"Ow!" Alden whimpered. She started shaking uncontrollably, not knowing how she was going to get away from them.

Then, seemingly out of nowhere, a cold wind swept up the alley and blew around them. Jewel gasped, and Chris's mouth dropped open. The frigid air was out of character for August, but Alden found it vaguely familiar. Confused, Jewel and Chris looked around the alley, searching for the source of the wind.

This was her chance! She kicked her foot toward Jewel and missed. Jewel's attention turned back to Alden, and she threw back her head and laughed. "Oh, tough girl, huh?"

Shaking with frustration, Alden couldn't fathom how to get Jewel off her. Then she remembered the first time she'd met Raccoon. Memories of their first encounter flooded back to her. Alden spit in Jewel's face.

"You slut!"

The cold draft was still swirling around them. Despite the warm evening, Alden's teeth were chattering. Suddenly, with a tremendous jolt, Jewel released Alden. Jewel's body lifted off the ground, flew backward, slammed against the far wall, and crumpled onto the ground.

Alden blinked, staring at her. What had just happened? Shaking the confusion from her head, Alden stumbled forward, determined to get away this time. Jewel screamed, "Stop her, Chris!"

Chris clutched her arm. Alden twisted and writhed, trying to break from his grasp. He pushed her, and she fell against the stage door. To her surprise, it opened easily, and she collapsed onto the cold concrete floor. Frantically, before Chris could reach her, she slammed the door shut and bolted it.

Trembling, Alden pulled herself up and leaned against the wall, sobbing. Trying to catch her breath, Alden stared at the stage door. She knew she had locked it when she'd left, but just now it had opened easily when she'd fallen against it. Alden turned around.

"Julie! What are you doing here?"

8

It is the secret of the world that all things subsist and do not die, but only retire a little from sight and return again. Nothing is dead; men feign themselves dead, and endure mock funerals and mournful obituaries, and there they stand, looking out the window, sound and well in some new strange disguise.

—RALPH WALDO EMERSON

I t was late October. The trees had turned their customary vibrant autumn colors. Leaves were raked into piles on neighborhood lawns or clogged drainage grates. Alden had started the ninth grade and was busy with nightly homework or studying for the debate club she had joined on impulse while daydreaming about her grandfather. She didn't miss her New York school, and she no longer dreaded the cafeteria. Her mother had bought her new clothes, but she'd grown two inches since they'd moved to Michigan, and already her jeans were too short. They were also baggy. She was thinner, more muscular, and toned. Still, not being able to let go of her old self-image, Alden preferred wearing oversized hoodies and shirts.

Alden and Julie hadn't talked about the night she'd escaped from Chris and Jewel through the stage door. She remembered Julie standing at the end of the hallway, her face stricken and pale. She'd thrown her arms around Alden and said, "Allie, are you all right?" They'd hidden in the entrance of the theatre, looking through the lobby doors for any further signs of Chris and Jewel. Standing close together in the lobby, watching for the enemy, Julie had held her hand and reassuringly patted Alden's back. Alden had been grateful she was there and knew that for the first time in her life, she had a best friend. An hour or so later, as dusk finally settled into late summer darkness, hoping her tormentors were long gone, Alden had slipped out the front lobby doors, run to the library, and swiftly biked home. Julie had assured Alden that her aunts were always running late and would be there shortly.

Explaining to Cleo why she was so late was almost as terrible as confronting Chris and Jewel. She didn't want Cleo or her mom to find out what had really happened. She knew that if her mom reported it to the police, it would only incite Chris and Jewel to retaliate. She didn't want to give up the freedom she had, coming and going from the theatre whenever she wanted. Alden hated keeping things from her mom, but in this case, she was better off not knowing. So, lamely, Alden had told Cleo she'd been with Walter and Julie in the theatre and had lost track of time. Cleo finally let it go, only after Alden promised never to forget her cell phone again.

Later, when the panic of that night had faded to anxiety about another confrontation with Chris and Jewel, Alden thought about Julie's aunts. Why had they been so late picking her up that evening?

Since school had started, Alden walked to school every day with Raccoon, who was repeating ninth grade.

"I'm taking art."

"You should be. You're good at it."

"The first time you saw my drawings, you said they were *grand*."

Alden giggled, remembering the embarrassing exchange. She'd hated Raccoon then. He was a little rough around the edges, but there was something appealing to her about him now.

"It's something my Grandpa Charlie used to say. '*Grand* debate, Alden,' or 'this has been a *grand* walk in the park'…you know."

"I never knew my grandfather."

Alden shifted her backpack on her shoulders. "How come you live with your uncle?"

"My mom left me and my dad when I was eight. I have no idea where she lives now. I don't remember her much, so I don't really care. My dad," Raccoon continued softly, "was a drunk…drugs too, I guess. He was in and out of rehab hospitals for a while. I'm sure that's why my mom couldn't take it anymore. I don't blame her for leaving, really. Then he landed in jail for armed robbery. That's when I went to live with my uncle."

"That sucks. Why does everybody call you Raccoon? That's not your real name, is it?"

He hesitated, his chin tilted, his jaw tight. Alden had learned that this was his way of closing off.

"Look, you don't have to tell me…"

Raccoon stopped and leaned on a stone wall next to the sidewalk. "My dad smacked me around when I was a kid, and sometimes I'd get black eyes, so all my friends started calling me Raccoon. You know… because raccoons have…" His voice trailed off.

Alden drew in a sharp breath. "God, that's horrible."

He shook his head. "No biggee."

They scuffed along in silence, kicking the fallen leaves out of their way. Softly, Alden asked, "What's your real name?"

"Alvin."

Alden swallowed, the corner of her lip twitching.

Raccoon blurted out, "I saw that! You're laughing! See, you're laughing!"

"I'm sorry, I can't help it!"

"I figured I'd better stick with Raccoon."

"You figured right!"

Raccoon playfully shoved her with his shoulder.

"Okay, okay," said Alden. "My turn. My middle name's Lucrecia, after my grandmother."

"Totally uncool. But you got off easy, 'cause it's your middle name."

"My grandfather went to school with a girl named Rosie Bottom."

Alden and Raccoon laughed even harder. They reached the corner of Maple and Oakdale, where Raccoon usually turned and Alden would continue on by herself.

"I'll walk you home," Raccoon said.

He was walking her home? Nervously she tucked her hair behind her ears, hoping he didn't notice how pleased she was with his offer.

"I'll never do that to my kids," Raccoon said after a while. "We gotta deal with enough shit. Parents gotta stick to names like Max or Gus."

It had been a rare moment of confession for Raccoon. Alden regarded him closely. She thought back to the first time they'd met in front of his house. His penetrating blue eyes hadn't changed, or the set of his jaw when he was challenged, but he seemed different now.

"Alden, there's something I gotta tell you. I told Chris to get lost. He's bad news."

Alden didn't reply.

"I heard what he and Jewel did to you. I'm sorry, man." Alden felt a surge of gratitude. Her gray eyes met his. "I don't know how you beat them down, but you've got a rep now, girl," he teased. "Jewel says she'll never go near the Pantages again. She says there's somethin' creepy about the place."

"Does everybody at school know?"

"You mean that nobody messes with Alden Proctor? Pretty much."

Warmed by his compliment, Alden blurted out, "Would you come to the theatre with me? I've told Walter and Julie all about you." Crap! She'd just admitted that she'd been talking about him. Had she said too much?

Raccoon stuffed his hands into his pockets and grinned at her. "Yeah, sure."

"Soon," she said.

"Soon," he answered.

The summer theatre camp had been so successful that classes continued into the fall with sessions after school and on Saturdays. Renovations of the Pantages had begun. The old seats were torn out and replaced with replicas of the original ones, the façade around the stage was repaired, and the walls were plastered and repainted. Alden often stopped by after school and watched the workers' progress with growing interest. Her mother met daily with Stan Gilmore, the project architect. They pored over old photographs of the interior, matching the details as best as they could. The workmen spent a great deal of time on the domed ceiling. Alden couldn't wait for them to repair the clouds and stars. The theatre was slowly being transformed. Walter had been right. In its day, the Pantages must have been spectacular.

One brisk fall evening, Alden, her mom, and Greg had finished one of Cleo's tasty dinners and settled comfortably in the family room. Alden liked Greg. More importantly, he liked her mom, and Alden hadn't seen her mom this happy in years. At the end of August, he'd taken Alden kayaking on Lake Michigan. They'd spent most of the day paddling along the shoreline, talking about New York, the Pantages, and Greg's adolescence growing up in Chicago. Later, they'd taken a quad buggy ride on the sand dunes. Afterward, windblown and covered with sand, Greg bought her ice cream at a roadside stand.

Now, her mom sipped her wine and said dreamily, "I wish I could do something at the Pantages that would bring in the rest of the capital. Everyone needs to see the work that's been done so far with the new seats and the painting."

"Why don't you do a performance?" suggested Alden. "You know, a vaudeville-type show, like Walter's always telling me about. You could have a headliner and a top banana, dancers—maybe a magician or a dog act."

"You know, Clare, that's not a bad idea," mused Greg.

Her mom nodded. "Vaudeville at the Pantages. I like it! We could show Smithfield what performances were really like in the old days! Alden, you're a genius." Her mom gathered her up in a big hug. "What if we turned the entire evening into the theatre's grand opening and set it in the 1920s? Antique cars, red carpet on the street in front of the theatre, and klieg lights spotlighting the sky!"

"She's on a roll!" said Greg.

"*Vaudeville comes back to the Pantages!*" her mom exclaimed enthusiastically.

"I bet you could get Jeremy and Chad, the guys who own WZBS, to cover the entire event live."

"I sat with them at the fundraiser," offered Alden. "They love the Pantages!"

"Fantastic idea. And, Alden, we'll also need Walter's help. He can suggest the type of acts to use in the show. I'm sure you guys can go through those old playbills and come up with tons of things! Any additional acts we need we can fill in with kids from the theatre camp." Her mom pulled Greg up off the couch. "This could bring in the rest of the money, Greg! With a vaudeville show, we might be able to convince the community the Pantages can thrive again, just as it used to. Maybe it will inspire people to reinvest in the downtown."

In November, the announcement of the spring vaudeville show kept Gina busy in the office, fielding phone calls. One Friday afternoon, Alden walked into the lobby, where groups of theatre-camp kids often congregated, happy to have the weekend ahead of her. Alden waved to Jenna and Meghan Friedman. Since the fundraiser back in June, they had become quite friendly.

"Hi, Alden," called Meghan in greeting.

"Hey. Got dance class?"

"Yeah. Jazz today," said Jenna.

More students arrived and took the stairs to the ballroom two at a time. Melody Reynolds, the girl Alden had tried to talk to last summer, walked in with two high school boys, a dance bag thrown carelessly over her shoulder.

"There he is," teased Meghan.

"Shut up," hissed Jenna, burying her face in her dance bag.

"My sister's hot for Garrett Ramsey, the guy with the Rasta hair. The other guy's Josh Gilmore."

Garrett and Josh were lost in Melody's smoky good looks, oblivious to Alden and the twins.

"Who's that?" Alden asked, nodding her head toward a boy leaning against the wall.

"Taylor McCord. He's new. He heard about the vaudeville show and joined the camp yesterday. Easy on the eyes, isn't he?"

"He's kinda weird, though," said Jenna. "He doesn't say much, and he's always staring."

Alden glanced at Taylor. He was watching her intently, as if he instinctively knew they were talking about him. Out of habit, Alden grabbed her sweater and tugged it down. Taylor's gaze darkened, as if challenging her to look away. Deliberately she broke eye contact with him. She turned back to the twins. "Are you guys going to audition for the show?"

"Yes!" said Meghan and Jenna simultaneously.

"What kind of act would you do?"

"Sing, dance…I just want to be in it!" Meghan exclaimed.

"I'm auditioning to sing a solo for the headliner spot," said Melody, joining them.

Remembering the last time she had tried to talk to Melody, Alden said cautiously, "Maybe they'll put in a number that'll feature all the camp students."

"Well, since your mom's the producer, you'll obviously be cast in the show."

"Oh, I'm not trying out."

"Oh, I get it. Your mom's just going to put you in the show without an audition."

"No," Alden answered hotly. "My mom's not like that. Besides, I…I couldn't get out there in front of all those people."

"Your loss." Melody spun around and headed up the stairs. Garrett and Josh rushed after her.

"Great. If she's auditioning, we'll never get a chance to be in it," said Jenna under her breath.

"Jenna's right," Meghan said fiercely. "Melody's fantastic. She'll probably get that headliner thing—whatever it is."

"They'll need other people too," Alden said with more confidence than she felt. Taylor McCord was still watching her.

"Right," Jenna said dejectedly. "Later, Alden." The twins grabbed their dance bags and trudged up the stairs.

Taylor pushed himself off the wall and moved toward her.

"Why do you let her get to you?"

"Who?"

"That Melody chick."

Was she that transparent? "I...I don't know. I just always seem to say the wrong thing around her."

"You're Alden Proctor, the development director's daughter."

"Yeah. So what?"

"So, is this vaudeville show really going to happen?"

"Of course, it is," Alden replied. "It has to. The show's going to reopen the Pantages."

"We'll see." Taylor stepped closer to Alden. She could feel his breath on her cheek. "Don't forget, Melody lacks style." Taylor casually turned and jogged up the stairs to the ballroom.

Baffled by Taylor's opinion of the usually popular Melody, Alden climbed the opposite staircase and went to her mother's office. It took her longer than usual to finish her math homework. Sighing, she shoved her binder into her backpack. Her mom came in and kissed her head.

"Hey, you. How was school?"

"Same old. Glad it's Friday. Where've you been?"

"I had a meeting with Stan in the theatre. They had to special-order a part for the motorized clouds." Her mom punched the buttons on her phone to pick up her voice mail. "Hmm," she said as she listened. She looked uneasy.

"What's up?" Alden asked.

"Not sure. Allie, I'm going to run over to city hall to see Mayor Klein for a bit. Do me a favor? Go to the archive room, and pull any newspaper reviews or articles about the acts that played the Pantages. I want our show to replicate vaudeville as much as possible. We need to get the right balance of comedians and singers versus novelty acts, like magicians and jugglers."

"Sure, I'll do it right now. Is Walter around?"

"No. He went over to the university to see if anyone in the theatre department wants to audition for the show. Meet you at home?"

Fifteen minutes later, Alden had articles and reviews from the *Smithfield Gazette* in a small pile on the desk, along with several old playbills. This should give her mother what she was looking for. She pushed the file cabinet drawer in, but it stuck, not closing all the way.

"Ugh!"

She pushed on it again. Something must be jammed in the back. Alden pulled the drawer all the way out and peered into the back of the cabinet. A yellowing file was caught in the track behind the drawer. Reaching behind the drawer, she managed to pull the file out with her fingertips. As she brought her arm out of the cabinet, her elbow hit the side of the metal track. Pain shot through her funny bone.

"Ow!" Alden dropped the file, and newspaper clippings spilled out onto the floor around her.

She bent down, gathering them up, her elbow stinging. Alden reached across the floor to retrieve an article that had fallen farther away than the others. She stared at the headline, dropping to her knees. Her fingers trembling, she picked up the clipping, barely able to grasp it.

Fourteen-Year-Old Falls to Her Death at Pantages

Alden sank onto the floor and leaned against the file cabinet for support. The article date rode above the headline—April 3, 1923. She forced her eyes away from the headline and read on.

Last night, fourteen-year-old Juliette Stanton fell from the balcony of the Pantages Theatre onto the aisle below. Efforts to revive her were attempted by a local physician in the audience but to no avail. Witnesses to the fall claimed Miss Stanton leaned out over the balcony in order to get a better view of the stage and lost her footing. An attempt was made to stop her fall by a nearby theatregoer, which failed.

Relatives say Miss Stanton was an avid fan of the Vaudeville and attended at least once a week. A dancer herself since the age of two, her favorite act at the Pantages was tap dancing. Juliette Stanton is survived by her parents and two brothers. Funeral services will be held at the Smithfield Funeral home two days from today.

Alden read the article a second time. Bile rose in her throat. Her heart was pounding, pulsating in her ears and temples. She attempted to stand up but sank to the floor again, her legs too weak to support her. Was it possible that this Juliette Stanton was a relative of Julie?

Alden's stomach churned, and nausea overcame her. Somehow she already knew the answer. She wasn't a relative. The girl in the article was the same Juliette Stanton. The same tap-dancing Julie. Her best friend was a ghost.

9

*When I see ghosts they look perfectly real and solid—
like a living human being. They are not misty; I can't see
through them; they don't wear sheets or bloody mummy
bandages. They don't have their heads tucked under their
arms. They just look like ordinary people, in living color,
and sometimes it is hard to tell who is a ghost.*

—Chris Woodyard, Haunted Ohio series

With the article clutched in her hand, Alden crawled to the desk and pulled herself up into the chair. She had wanted to know if the rumors were true, if the Pantages really had a ghost—but not that it was Julie!

She didn't know anything about ghosts, how they appeared or disappeared or how they managed to be lifelike and in human form. But Alden knew in her gut that Julie wasn't alive. Suddenly so many things began to make sense. The tapping noises she had first heard in the theatre, the strange, muffled voices. It was always cold when Julie was around! Did the cold air have something to do with death? She shuddered.

Alden was not only horrified but also felt foolish. She had been duped and played! Why hadn't Julie told her? Was there some reason why she couldn't reveal the truth? They were friends—or at least she thought they were—and friends trusted each other. *Stupid, stupid me!* Alden felt betrayed, but she couldn't understand why it mattered so much. She'd fallen for every lie Julie had told her. And who were these so-called aunts? Alden gasped. The Gleason sisters—found dead the morning after they opened their act at the Pantages! Was it possible the Gleason sisters also haunted the Pantages?

Her head throbbed. She stumbled over to the open cabinet drawer. Her fingers fumbled through the manila files as she searched for the one labeled with Walter's handwriting. She knew the critic's review of the Gleason sisters' act was missing, but maybe there was something else she could find. Walter! Did *he* know that Julie was a ghost? Alden's fingers paused on top of the files. "I think there are several ghosts in the Pantages," he'd told her. Had he known? Had Walter lied to her as well? Hot tears ran down Alden's face as she slammed the file cabinet shut.

The warm August evening of Alden's fight in the alley with Chris and Jewel came rushing back to her. The alley had suddenly become cold, the draft swirling around them. Chris and Jewel had noticed it, too. How had Jewel ended up in a heap against the alley wall? That night, she'd left through the stage door and checked to see that it was locked. Yet when Chris pushed her against the door, it had opened easily. The backstage hallway had been freezing, and Julie had been standing at the end of it. Rooted next to the filing cabinet, Alden trembled with confusion.

TAP…tap…tap…tap, tap, tap, tap, **TAP**, tap, tap. The familiar sound was coming from the stage.

Alden's legs shook. She bent over, hands on her knees, trying to calm herself. She heard the tapping again. She had to find out. She had to know the truth! Gripping the article in her hand, she raced down the hallway, through the wings, and onto the stage.

Julie stopped, her foot poised in midair, and looked at Alden's anguished face. Her eyes traveled from Alden to the newspaper article in her hand. She froze.

"Is this you?" Alden cried, shaking the newspaper article. Julie stared at the clipping in Alden's hand. "'Last night, fourteen-year-old Juliette Stanton fell from the balcony of the Pantages Theatre onto the aisle below?'" quoted Alden from the first line, her voice hollow.

"Allie, I…" Julie reached toward her, but Alden stumbled backward.

"Just tell me the truth, Julie!" Alden demanded. "Is this you? Are you…are you…?"

Julie stared in dismay at Alden and didn't reply, her silence an admission of the truth that Alden was so desperate to learn but too frightened to hear.

"Are you the same Juliette Stanton who's in this article?" Her voice was breaking now. "Tell me!"

"Yes! Yes, it's me!" Julie blurted out. "I'm a…I'm a ghost."

Alden coughed as she tried to hold back the sobs constricting her tightening chest. She could hardly breathe.

"I'm sorry I didn't tell you. I should have, I know."

"I thought you were my friend, Julie, but you lied to me. I thought…"

"Please, you *have* to understand…I *couldn't* tell you the truth."

Alden spun away and started toward the wings. She had to get away. She wished she'd never found the newspaper article!

"Alden, wait! Please…" Julie cried. Alden paused but refused to look at her. Haltingly, Julie continued, "I couldn't tell you because…I didn't think you'd ever believe me…or *it*…I mean, believe what I *was*…what I *am*." She was stumbling over herself, the words pouring haphazardly out of her mouth. "And I…I wanted to dance."

Alden jerked around, gasping at Julie in disbelief. Was that the only reason Julie hadn't told her she was a ghost? Because she wanted to *dance*? Had Julie kept it a secret from her, pretending to be her friend so she would introduce her to Walter?

Sucking in a rasping breath, Julie rushed on. "I'm not explaining this very well. I didn't mean just *dance*…" She swallowed, taking in large gulps of air, slowing herself down. "I didn't want to tell you because I…I wanted a friend so badly. It's been so lonely here, and when *you* came to the theatre, and we met…" Julie stopped. She was hiccupping violently. She struggled to go on. "I thought if I told you the truth, you'd think I was some kind of freak. I thought you'd be too frightened of me." Julie gathered the front of her dress in her fists, clenching and unclenching the fabric in her fingers, her face as twisted as her dress. "I'll understand if you can't be friends with me anymore."

Alden was having trouble grasping what—or whom, she thought with horror—Julie really was. Taking Alden's silence as negative confirmation,

Julie sank to the edge of the stage, wiping the tears off her face. She tilted her head up and looked out into the house of the Pantages. Slowly, Alden sat down next to her. She had to hear the truth. She had to hear Julie's explanation, however strange and terrifying it might be.

"Julie…you're dead? You're…a ghost?"

Julie swallowed, her eyes darting around the theatre, taking in the balcony, the candelabra, and the domed ceiling. She seemed to be gathering strength from what she saw.

"Yes."

"But how can that be? You're sitting right next to me. You seem alive. You're flesh, you're…a person."

"I know, it's hard to believe, but I'm a ghost." Julie turned and looked at Alden, her eyes focused intensely on her. "I'm dead, Alden. I died in this theatre when I fell off the balcony. But instead of disappearing from the earth like most people do when they die, my spirit was still connected to something earthly, and I couldn't leave. I'm trapped between life and normal death. I crossed over into death, but not into the spiritual world. I'm earthbound because I was connected to this place…to the Pantages. I'm a theatre ghost."

Earthbound. Forever tied to the Pantages as a ghost. Alden was overcome by a tremendous sense of loss. The pain was the same as the ache she'd felt when Grandpa Charlie had died. "I wish you'd told me."

"I know," Julie whispered.

"I don't get it. How come I can see you and touch you? How come you're not some floating, transparent shape?"

"Theatre ghosts can *choose* to be seen in human form by living people—or as we like to call you, 'Alives.' We can appear using this lifelike persona."

"Can all ghosts choose to be seen in human form?"

"Yes, but *theatre* ghosts do it better than other ghosts because we've been trained," Julie bragged. "In life, we were performers. In death as earthbound ghosts, we know how to appear as something we once were. But if we show ourselves, we have to choose carefully. Passing yourself off as an Alive can get tricky."

"Why?"

"Theatre ghosts have made mistakes and gotten caught. Luckily, Alives have never been able to actually prove we exist. You see, to the living, theatre ghosts are a legend people tell and retell. They describe sightings of us and joke about the mystery of it all. But if an untrustworthy Alive were to actually reveal us to the living, we'd vanish from the earth. It's why we have to be so careful when we choose to show ourselves."

Julie's voice trailed off. Her eyes rested on the ghost light standing at center stage, casting its familiar shadows around the theatre. "I had to show myself to *you*, Allie. I chose you 'cause I wanted to be your friend. Then, when I met you, I knew you wouldn't expose me to the Alive world."

"Never," Alden whispered. She was suddenly frightened. The reality of what Julie was telling her was sinking in. "No one is going to expose you," Alden said firmly. "The Pantages is your home! This place is…" Alden remembered the first time she had entered the theatre through the black-and-gold doors and the joy that filled her every time she walked down the aisle or stood on the stage. "The Pantages is special. I could feel it the first time I came here. We've got to do everything we can to keep you safe!"

Julie lay back on the stage and looked up at the midnight-blue ceiling. "When I was little, I used to come to the Pantages all the time to watch the vaudeville. To be here—to be part of it—was the most thrilling and, at the same time, the most comforting place I could be. I wanted to be a hoofer on the vaudeville circuit more than anything. Every spare moment I had, I'd spend in dance lessons. Kids used to make fun of me in school. They'd say I was star struck and obsessed. They called me a dingbat. I guess," Julie admitted, "I knew I wasn't like the other kids. They didn't have to tell me." Alden knew all too well. "The Pantages was the only place I could go and…escape. I always felt at home here. I'd watch the acts, and everything outside the theatre would temporarily go away."

Hesitantly Alden asked, "What happened when you…when you fell?"

"I don't know! It was just so stupid. Harvey, the magician, was performing his act, and the O'Conners were up next. They were my favorite dance team. Oh Alden, if you could have seen them dance! He would lift her up, and she'd soar in the air and drop back into his arms, never missing a step." Julie was crying again. "That night...I knew the O'Conners would be waiting backstage, ready to come on. So I leaned out over the balcony railing to see if I could see them in the wings. But I leaned too far and lost my hold on the railing. I...I was just so careless!" Julie angrily brushed at the dampness on her face.

Alden reached over and squeezed Julie's hand. Gently she asked, "Were you with your parents?"

"I attended the vaudeville that night with my older brother, Jasper. It wasn't his fault, really. He fancied a girl who worked in the concession stand in the lobby."

"You mean Jasper wasn't with you in the balcony that night? He was in the lobby?"

Julie nodded her head. "I don't blame him, Alden. I was old enough to watch by myself. It was just...dumb."

"No," said Alden. "It was an accident. You just got caught up in the show and excitement of it all." After a minute, Alden confided, "I wish the fall hadn't happened to you, Julie, but if it hadn't..." She couldn't continue, afraid to reveal what she was really thinking.

"I would never have met you," Julie finished for her.

Alden tried to smile at her but managed only a grimace. The strangeness of the circumstances were sinking in. "Julie, the article said your accident happened in 1923. You've been at the Pantages as a ghost all these years?"

"Yes."

"After all this time, how can you still be fourteen years old?"

"Theatre ghosts stay the same age they were when they died."

"So you've been fourteen all this time? You've never gotten older?" Alden was having trouble grasping this.

"Well, I'm already dead. I can't grow old and die again!" Julie said, giggling.

"I guess so." Slowly Alden ventured, "What happened *after* you fell?"

"I heard voices asking my name and saw the ghost light shining in my eyes. I realized the light was shining on me. They gathered around me, shook my hand, and welcomed me."

"Who were they?"

"Other theatre ghosts. Foster Simon and his brother Rascal, from the Fox Theatre in Atlanta, and Ida Murphy and Geraldine Gaynor from the Palace Theatre in New York. They showed up when I died because I instantly became a part of the vaudeville circuit."

"But vaudeville died. Theatres haven't had vaudeville shows for almost a century."

Julie jumped up, the shadows caused by the light crossing her face. She seemed to breathe in the soul of the theatre, her eyes shining. "Our vaudeville shows never ended. We perform under the glow of the ghost light."

The ghosts performed their acts when the theatre was empty. The ghost light legend was true!

"Don't you see, Alden? When I died, I became a ghost, but I finally got my chance to dance in vaudeville! We're all performers and stagehands on the *ghost* vaudeville circuit. Theatre ghosts perform all over the country. We've been waiting years for the Pantages to reopen so that we can perform here again."

"You leave the Pantages?" It hadn't occurred to Alden that ghosts could travel.

"Sure. There're old vaudeville theatres in all the big cities—Minneapolis, Saint Louis, Schenectady. Ghosts can teleport to another location in seconds. It's called 'think and blink.'" Julie laughed. "I know it sounds funny, but we close our eyes and concentrate on the theatre we want to travel to, and then we blink—and we're there! When I first started, the circuit manager didn't let me go without Gloria and Irene, but now I travel with Foster and Rascal or Ida and sometimes Geraldine. After each performance, we return to our home theatres."

"Who do you perform for?"

"Other ghosts. That's my only regret. I wish I could have performed for a live audience, especially my mother."

"Are there enough ghosts to fill a theatre?"

"There're twenty or more ghosts to every Alive. We always outnumber the living. And ghosts love to be entertained! Our ghost shows are just like the real vaudeville. It's why I first told you I wanted to study tap with

Walter. If I improve my act, maybe someday I can become a headliner."
Julie paused and then said softly, squeezing Alden's hands, "I was lucky,
because at the same time...I got to know you." Alden's eyes filled with
tears.

"Does Walter know?" Alden asked.

"I'm not sure. Sometimes I wonder if he might suspect."

A gust of cold air blew across the stage, and the ghost light flickered.
A clattering of high heels on the spiral staircase and the sound of dis-
agreeing voices broke the silence.

"What's that?" Alden asked.

"The other ghosts who live here."

10

Truly the universe is full of ghosts, not sheeted churchyard specters, but the inextinguishable elements of individual life, which having once been, can never die, though they blend and change, and change again forever.

—H. RIDER HAGGARD, KING SOLOMON'S MINES

"I thought I told you to hide those newspaper articles!"

"I did, Gloria. I didn't think she'd find them."

"You should have found a better hiding place. Now look what's happened, Irene!"

"It's too late now," came a gravelly voice. "Let's just meet the little lady."

Uneasily, Alden watched as two women reached the bottom of the spiral stairs and breezed toward them. They were obviously sisters. Their faces were perfect ovals, and they had dark-brown eyes and heart-shaped lips painted bright red. They wore low-waisted floral frocks, white cotton gloves, and bright-colored hats that fit tightly against their heads, their short, brown hair sticking out from under the brims. The two women were followed by a man in overalls. He had messy red hair and only one arm.

"Alden, we're truly sorry you had to find out about us in this way," said the older of the two women.

"It's my fault, really," the other said. "I should have disposed of those old newspaper articles instead of trying to hide them."

The man deftly unwrapped a peppermint round with one hand and popped it into his mouth. Julie pulled Alden toward the curious trio.

"Alden, this is Gloria and Irene Gleason."

Nervously, Alden shook their hands. "Um…hi. Hello," Alden stuttered.

"And this," Julie continued, "is Red."

Red took her hand and shook it. When he pulled away, there was a peppermint in Alden's palm. She laughed softly. "Thanks, Red."

"Now," chirped Gloria, pulling off her gloves and touching Alden's cheek, "we don't want you to be upset with Juliette for not telling you about us. She did the right thing when she chose you." Gloria pulled a dainty embroidered handkerchief out of her clutch purse and dabbed at Alden's eyes.

"And we know," Irene chimed in, "that you aren't the type of Alive who would expose her."

"Oh no," said Alden. "I'd never do that." She looked at the Gleason sisters and Red. "*You've* chosen me, too?"

"Well, of course, dear," said Gloria. "We know you'll keep our secret."

"Julie is quite a little hoofer, isn't she?" said Irene proudly.

"But I'm not a headliner like you two."

"Only a matter of time, dear," Irene said confidently.

"So, you all live here too…at the Pantages?"

"Home, sweet home," bragged Red.

"Are there any others?" Alden asked, trying to grasp the fact that there were four ghosts standing in front of her.

Gloria, Red, and Julie exchanged a worried glance. Irene muttered, "There is another one of us, but he never shows himself. He is disgruntled, to say the least. Imagine, hiding from everyone for decades."

Gloria nudged her sister. "This is all silly talk. No need to bother Alden with it."

"It's no bother," said Alden. "I want to meet all of—"

A loud noise, like microwave popcorn rapidly exploding at the same time, made Alden momentarily forget about the absent Pantages ghost. Pop. Pop. Pop. POP! POP! POP! "What's that?" Alden asked, looking around wildly.

"That's just Kean arriving," explained Gloria.

The popping grew louder. As the noise reached its peak, there was a loud crack and a flickering light, and a man walked through the back theatre wall. He wore a dark suit and hat and had an overcoat thrown over his arm. With the addition of spats over his shoes, he looked like a fashion model from the early nineteen hundreds.

"Gloria! Irene! Have you lost track of the time?" the man said, brushing dust off his trousers. He clasped Red's one hand. "How are ya, Red?"

"Couldn't be better, Mr. Thomas."

"That's Kean Thomas," Julie whispered to Alden. "He's a singer and the manager of our ghost vaudeville show. He's in charge of booking the acts in the different theatres on the circuit. His home is New York's Shubert Theatre."

Kean glided over to Gloria and Irene. "Don't both of you look ravishing!" he said, kissing their hands. Irene flushed. Gloria's laugh was like a tinkling bell as she playfully swatted Kean's hand away.

"He's a notorious flirt and ladies' man," Julie whispered more loudly so that Kean could overhear her. "The circuit ghosts gossip that he's got a girl in every city."

Kean turned and approached Alden. Sweeping off his hat, he gave Alden a teasing formal bow. "And who is this beautiful young lady?"

"Oh Kean," scolded Julie. "It's Alden Proctor. I've told you all about her." She turned to Alden. "Kean's a great singer, Allie. When he was alive, the women in the audience used to swoon, and then they'd line up at the stage door to get his autograph."

"Ah, gone are the days," Kean said wistfully. He gave Juliette a brilliant grin. "Alden, did you know Miss Juliette is a heartbreaker? She says I'm too old for her, but I keep trying to change her mind." He winked at Alden as Julie teasingly shoved him.

"You...you walked through the wall," Alden stammered.

"Well, yes," stated Kean. "Juliette, didn't you tell her?"

Julie was laughing at Alden's shocked face. "Sorry, I didn't get around to it. Alden," she said matter-of-factly, "ghosts can walk through walls—that part of the legend is true. Kean teleported here from New York."

Kean pulled a pocket watch out of his vest. "The company of such beautiful ladies is taking my mind off my job. The girls and I are booked at the Folly Theater in Kansas City and need to be off."

"Oh yes, we're all a flurry," Gloria gushed, closing her pocketbook and pulling her gloves back on.

Irene appealed to Red. "Look after Julie while we're gone, won't you, Red?"

Red tossed Julie a peppermint. "I always do, Miss Gleason."

Kean threw on his overcoat and explained to Alden, "I have to be there early before George Templeton arrives with his entourage. If his dressing room isn't prepared according to his contract to the last dotted *I* and crossed *T*, I'll hear about it."

"Oh, that man," sputtered Irene.

"George Templeton's an acrobat, whose act was famous at the Palace in New York," Julie explained to Alden. "He's rather difficult."

"That's an understatement," said Kean.

Julie hugged Gloria and Irene and waved at Kean. "I'll see you when you get back."

Kean took Alden's hand and leaned down to kiss it.

"Come on, Tiger." Irene pulled Kean's collar and dragged him toward the back wall of the theatre. They stopped briefly, fiercely concentrating. There was a flash of light, and then the Gleason sisters and Kean walked through the wall. The popping noise began again, loudly this time, and then faded away.

"And I've got work to do up on the catwalk," Red said, looking up into the fly loft. "I keep thinking if I repair all the lighting instruments, the Pantages might join the circuit again." He looked at Alden, his eyes filled with hope. "Now that you and your mom are here, maybe that's possible." He popped another peppermint into his mouth and strolled toward the spiral staircase.

"See ya, Red," called Julie.

As soon as the ghosts left, Alden missed them immediately. They were fascinating in their own quirky ways. "They're incredible, Julie."

"Gloria and Irene died only a few years before I did. I was so scared when I first crossed into death. I missed my family, and they kind of... adopted me. That's why I call them my aunts. Red's been here the longest.

When Gloria and Irene are traveling, and I'm not booked, he kinda looks out for me."

"Anybody out here?" called Walter from the hallway.

Alden and Julie jumped and turned toward the wings. Walter walked out on the stage, his expression curious. Alden wondered if her eyes were still swollen from crying. Walter picked up the newspaper clipping from the floor. Alden had forgotten it! It must have dropped out of her hand when she had run out onto the stage. The two girls nervously looked at each other.

Walter read the headline and glanced up at them. The girls locked hands. Walter read the article, slowly raised his head, and stared—first at Julie and then at Alden.

"I found that article in the back of the filing cabinet," whispered Alden.

"So it's true." Slowly, Walter crossed toward Julie. "Juliette Stanton," he said with old-fashioned formality, "I hope you've found your stay here pleasurable. I trust the Pantages has been a good home for you."

"You knew?" Alden gasped.

"No, but I had a hunch," he said. "Tell me, Miss Stanton, do you *really* perform shows when the theatre is empty?"

"Under the ghost light!" Julie laughed. "And if I keep studying with you, I might become a headliner."

"I'm sure you will, my dear." Walter snapped his fingers. "Speaking of headliners, Alden, Artie Rosenberg is going to direct our show. He's the head of the university theatre department and is a vaudeville historian."

Julie stared at Alden and Walter. "You're putting on a show? Here, at the Pantages?"

"My mom's going to produce an authentic vaudeville show as a fund-raiser for the reopening of the theatre."

"Just like the old days," added Walter.

Alden was studying Julie. "Is that okay, Julie? It'll be a good thing for the Pantages to reopen, won't it?"

"Am I okay?" Julie's face was ecstatic. "Why, this is fantastic!"

Alden and Walter exchanged confused looks.

"Don't you see? If you reopen the Pantages, it means the ghost vaude-ville show can reopen here too!" Julie's eyes were shining, her hands trem-bling with excitement. "I have an even better idea. If I could be in *your* show, I'd finally get my chance to dance in front of an audience of Alives, not just ghosts."

Walter said slowly, "I'm not sure you can be *in* it, Julie."

Her face fell. "Why not?"

Alden agreed. "Julie, how can we be sure there wouldn't be someone who'd find out you're a ghost and expose you to the world?"

"Could that happen?" asked Walter.

"Yes," Alden explained. "And if someone did, she'd cease to exist."

Walter said sternly to Julie, "I'm not sure we can take that chance."

Julie's face fell, and for the second time that afternoon, she began cry-ing. "It's all I ever wanted…to dance on this stage and hear the applause of Alives." Julie sank to the floor and buried her head in her hands.

Walter bent down, putting his hand on her shoulder. "I'm sure there's a way you could help us with the show," he offered. "You know more than any of us about vaudeville. You can help choose the acts, make costumes, and props."

"Wait a sec," Julie looked up, her eyes glistening impishly. "What if people didn't know it was me? I mean, what if they thought the performer was someone else, but it was really me?"

Walter's eyes narrowed. "What are you getting at?"

Julie leaped up, the excitement back in her voice. "What if Alden did it? She could be the tap-dancing act in the show, but on the night of the performance, I would take her place. We're the same height and have the same coloring."

Alden couldn't believe what Julie was suggesting. "First of all, I don't tap dance well enough!"

Julie cut her off, pacing back and forth and slapping her hands together. "Sure you do. You're getting better every day. We'll just have to step up the lessons."

"And second," Alden persisted, "there's going to be a director and rehearsals. I don't know anything about performing. I can't get up in front of people."

Julie grabbed Alden's hands. "You could do it, Allie! I'll help you. You just have to have a routine that's good enough to make the show and attend a few rehearsals. Then I'd take over. We could use your final dress rehearsal as a test run."

"Julie, we'd never get away with it!" Alden looked at Walter helplessly. He shrugged, a smile tugging at his mouth.

"Please, Alden. Please? For me?"

"I don't know…" Alden looked at Julie's eager face: Juliette Stanton, ghost of the Pantages. How lonely she must have been, living as a ghost in the theatre for decades, with only her dream of performing to sustain her. Alden couldn't imagine that kind of existence. Julie seemed confident she could make this scheme work. "Sure…piece of cake," Alden thought sarcastically. Out loud, she said, sighing, "Oh, all right. I'll do it."

"Hooray!" Julie grabbed Alden and spun her around.

Walter chuckled. "I guess we've got some work to do."

Instead of celebrating the plan with them, Alden had a sinking feeling she couldn't shake.

11

Be slow to fall into friendship; but when thou art in, continue firm and constant.

—SOCRATES

As soon as Alden agreed to Julie's plan, she immediately regretted it. First, she had to audition, and even if she made it, she'd have to go through all the rehearsals with people watching and scrutinizing her. Second, if Alden and Julie were to switch places for the dress rehearsal and performance, wouldn't people realize that it wasn't Alden dancing—especially her mother? Julie had assured her that with costumes, lighting, and the vastness of the theatre, no one in the audience would be able to tell the difference. But what if something went terribly wrong? What if an Alive caught on, discovered that Julie was a ghost, and tried to expose her?

Since she had made the discovery of Julie's true identity, Alden had learned that the temperature always dropped when ghosts were nearby; they could turn lights on and off, they cried and hiccupped and sneezed, and they had the ability to love. She wished she could make Julie an Alive again. Instead, she painfully realized, Julie was a ghost who'd never gotten her show-business break—a chance to dance in front of a live audience. So even though it was risky, Alden knew she had to go along with Julie's plan. She was determined to make Julie's dream real. She would audition. Hopefully she would get into the show. They would switch places for the dress rehearsal and performance. She would do it for Julie.

Alden decided not to tell her mother about Julie. She rationalized that withholding the truth from her mom would protect Julie better. Walter had agreed that secrecy was right—at least for now. The fewer people who knew Julie was a ghost, the better.

Several weeks later, Alden got home from school to find her mother and Greg deep in conversation.

"What are we going to do, Greg? We've come so far!"

Alden dropped her book bag on the floor. "Mom?"

"It's the Pantages, honey. We've had a setback. Remember when I told you that Harold Brennan tried to buy the Pantages a year ago, but the city council agreed not to sell it to him, hoping that enough money could be raised to reopen the theatre?"

"Yeah."

"Today," her mom said, sighing heavily, "Brennan sweetened the offer he originally made to the city. Mayor Klein hinted to me that this might happen a few weeks back."

"Whatever deal he wants to make can't help Smithfield as much as your plans for the Pantages," Alden said confidently.

"He's doubled his offer for the property, and he's willing to pay the back taxes that have been owed to the city since the theatre closed."

"But Brennan wants to tear the theatre down! Why would he spend so much money on a building he wants to destroy?"

"He doesn't care about the theatre," Greg said. "This is about winning."

"Mom, we can't let him do this!"

"Clare," asked Greg, "what about your application to make the Pantages a historic landmark?"

"There's been a problem with that application as well." The bitterness in her voice was apparent. "The paperwork I filed has been held up by Senator Gionardi. It doesn't mean it won't eventually happen, but for right now, the approval's been stalled."

"Let me guess," Greg said. "Brennan's given money to Gionardi's reelection campaign."

"Bingo. Apparently he's made sizable contributions. Of course, I only *suspect* Gionardi's been paid off. I don't have any proof."

"But if the city accepts Brennan's latest offer, he can tear down the theatre while the landmark application's stalled," Alden said numbly.

"That's right. I'm so sorry, Alden. I know you've come to really love the place. The only good news is that I was able to convince Mayor Klein to hold the city council off from considering Brennan's offer until after the vaudeville show."

Alden felt a glimmer of hope. "All the more reason to make it a huge success."

"This fight isn't over, either," Greg said. "I think WZBS needs a tip on the possible bribery of a state politician. Jeremy and Chad are friends of mine. I'll make the call."

Alden was shaken. Her mother was fighting for the very existence of Julie's home. Now that Alden knew the Pantages had ghost occupants, it was more important than ever to save the theatre.

The next day, Alden was in the theatre putting on her tap shoes when the stage suddenly got colder.

"Up here, Miss Alden." She looked up into the dark fly loft, recognizing Red's gravelly voice. "Come on up."

Alden scrambled to her feet and ran up the spiral stairs to the catwalk. Red was tightening a clamp on a lighting instrument, sucking on his customary peppermint.

"I had these lights working a couple of weeks ago, but for some reason they aren't working again. Funny." Red slipped the wrench into his pocket and looked down at the stage. "In my opinion, the best view of the vaudeville is from up here. Somethin' 'bout hearing the music rise up from the pit, watching the acts from up here—it's mighty special." Feeling a bit queasy from the height, Alden grasped tightly to the railing.

"Yep, spent forty years here. Started working backstage the year the Pantages first opened. I was ten years old."

"You must love the Pantages as much as Julie does," said Alden.

"Gave my arm and my life to the place."

"What happened?"

"A backdrop got caught on a lighting fixture as the stagehands were flying it into place. I climbed up on this railing and tried to fix it so the show could continue. I slipped. My arm got tangled up in the ropes. Ripped my arm right off, and I kept falling."

"How awful!"

Red chuckled. "It's how I got my nickname—One-Armed Red. Sorta proud of it, now. It's like a badge of honor. The show must go on and all that."

"I'm grateful you chose to show yourself to me."

"Thanks aren't necessary. We're just happy to see the Pantages reopen. The ghosts need to add this theatre to their circuit. It's important to all of us." Red looked at his pocket watch. "Well, I gotta run. Been called to Minneapolis. Spotlight needs fixin'." Red walked to the end of the catwalk, paused, and, with a flash of light, walked through the wall. The smell of peppermint lingered in the air.

Alden clicked down the staircase in her tap shoes. She drilled her audition for the show over and over, her feet slamming into the floor, trying to tap away her worries about the future of the Pantages. Some of the steps were intricate, but Alden was slowly getting the hang of it. She felt looser and lighter on her feet. Later, with sweat trickling down her back, Alden turned the music off on her phone and grabbed a towel from her dance bag.

"Bravo, bravo."

Alden spun around. Taylor was lounging in a seat halfway up the aisle, his legs hanging over the seat in front of him.

"How long have you been here?" she demanded.

"Long enough." Taylor strode down the aisle toward her. "That's a pretty good routine. I thought you weren't auditioning."

"I wasn't. But I…I changed my mind."

"A vaudeville show should always have a good tap number," Taylor said, jumping up onto the stage next to Alden.

"Really? I mean, if I get in, I don't want people to think it's because of my mom."

"If you get in, it's 'cause you're good."

Alden threw her towel into her dance bag, blushing from the compliment. "What are you auditioning with?"

"I'm a magician. I make things disappear."

"I hope the show's a success."

Taylor's eyes narrowed. "Why?"

"Because I want the Pantages to be here always. I want it to reopen and not be torn down. Don't you?"

"Yeah, sure."

Alden wasn't sure she believed him.

"Speaking of disappearing, I gotta cut out. See you at auditions."

"Right. Um...hey, Taylor?"

"Yeah?"

"I hope your magic act gets into the show too."

"It will." Taylor left abruptly, leaving Alden to shake her head at his odd behavior.

Saturday morning, Alden got out of bed and looked out the window. The sky was brightening. Raccoon was meeting her in half an hour— he'd finally agreed to come to the Pantages and meet Walter and Julie. Alden had promised Julie that Raccoon was a trustworthy Alive and that she could show herself to him. Her ghost identity would be kept from Raccoon...at least for now.

Alden pulled on a pair of jeans and looked down in dismay. They were getting too short again. At least she kept growing up, not out. Alden took extra time with her hair, putting in some extra time brushing, even spray-ing, but she still couldn't get it to look right. She stared at herself in the mirror. She never used to care what her hair looked like. Was she doing this for Raccoon? Plus—she was anxious. What was going on with her?

Dismissing the uncertainty, she pulled her hair into a ponytail and ran downstairs to meet Raccoon. They walked quickly, covering the few blocks to the downtown area without saying much. The wind off Lake Michigan was so cold it made it difficult to talk. They arrived shivering at the stage door.

They found Walter and Julie in the wings. "So you're Raccoon," Walter said, shaking his hand. "I was beginning to think you didn't really exist. Welcome."

Raccoon smiled at Julie. "And you must be the incredible tap dancer."

Julie flushed. "Thanks, but Alden exaggerates."

"Not likely," Raccoon said proudly. "Alden always tells the truth, sometimes even when you don't wanna to hear it." Alden met his blue eyes with a half smile and then quickly looked away. Julie was watching them curiously.

"Raccoon, we're going to be hanging scenery for the show, and I'm not as strong as I used to be," confessed Walter. "I could use someone like you to help weight the lines with sandbags. You up for it?"

"I am."

"I hear you're an artist."

"I can't guess who told you that," Raccoon said sarcastically, gently shoving Alden. She playfully shoved him back. "Yes, I'm an artist," he answered straightforwardly. "*An artist.* I like the sound of that."

"Would you help me with the painting as well?"

"I'm in," said Raccoon.

"Then you're officially a theatre kid," Walter pronounced.

"Not sure how my uncle will feel about that."

"Time will tell. Now, grab that sandbag, and we'll get started."

Raccoon gave Alden a smile, hefted the bag onto his shoulder, and followed Walter.

Julie pulled Alden onto the stage. "He's cute, Alden. Do you like him?"

"Shh." Alden glanced at Raccoon in the wings. "We're friends."

"Right," Julie chided knowingly. Then she whispered, "I have news. Because your mom is reopening the theatre with your vaudeville show, the ghosts are putting the Pantages back on the ghost circuit."

"You mean they're coming here to do a show?"

"Under the ghost light on the same night as yours," Julie answered happily. "They've been waiting for years for this. Kean will be here, and Ida Murphy, and I can't wait for you to meet Foster and Rascal. They're fantastic tap dancers, and Rascal's…well, he's just that—a rascal. Of course, we'll have to tolerate George Templeton!"

"What's with him, anyway?" Alden asked.

"He's impossible!" exclaimed Julie. "His dressing room is never big enough, his costumes aren't cleaned right, he doesn't like his place on the bill. He gets the other performers riled up, too. Kean's threatened to quit managing the ghost circuit because of him. I don't think he will though. He loves it too much."

"Why don't you just ask Templeton not to perform or...or...fire him? Can you do that?"

Julie shook her head. "Nope. His act's too good, too important to the circuit. In fact, he's spectacular. Ghosts tell me that when George was alive, audiences went wild!"

"How'd he die?"

"On stage at the Palace. He was walking the high wire, misjudged a trick, and fell and broke his neck." Alden shuddered. "Wait till you see Gloria and Irene juggle. They're unbelievable!"

The thought of seeing the Pantages filled with ghosts from theatres all over the country made Alden giddy. "Can I really meet all of them?" she asked.

"Sure. You've been cleared as trustworthy by all the ghosts. Here's the best part—you're invited to our dress rehearsal. You'll come, won't you?"

"Of course!"

"Come on," Julie said. "Let me see your routine."

Nervously, Alden tugged on her shirt. The auditions were the next day.

He who seeks only for applause from without
has all his happiness in another's keeping.

—Oliver Goodsmith

Alden sank down in her seat, clutching her tap shoes against her chest. Hopeful singers, dancers, jugglers, magicians, and stand-up comedians filled the theatre, anxiously scrutinizing each other, discussing their music, and giggling with nervous anticipation.

"Did you see the director? What about the choreographer? How many people are they casting?"

Alden sat alone, isolated from the others. These people had been through this before. She'd only been working with Walter and Julie for a few months. She wished she'd had more time. At her last rehearsal, Walter had watched her audition and told Alden that she was ready. She'd run through the routine ten times that day, until she was dripping with sweat, her muscles quivering with exhaustion.

"Alden, it's marvelous! You've come a long way," Walter had said.

"You dance this well at the tryouts, and you're sure to get cast," Julie added.

Alden bit her thumbnail. All the preparation wouldn't help her if she fell apart at the audition. The director, Artie Rosenberg, was on the stage, going through the audition list with her mom. Alden slid farther down in her seat. She wished she were invisible. Maybe they would forget she was here and never call her name. Or maybe she could ask her mother to remove her audition paperwork. Then she wouldn't have to go through with it. Why had she allowed Julie to talk her into this? She had never danced in front of anyone except Julie and Walter!

Alden watched Melody talking quietly with Garrett and Josh on the other side of the theatre. Melody flipped her curly hair off her shoulders and studied her sheet music, her face confident and focused. Taylor sat on the edge of the stage alone, watching silently.

"Hi, Alden." Meghan and Jenna hurried into the row behind her and flopped down. Meghan leaned over the back of the seats and whispered, "Are you excited?"

"I guess so."

"I'm nervous," said Jenna. "I just wanna spot in the chorus, but look at all the people here!"

"I heard Melody practicing her song yesterday afternoon. She's freaking awesome," Meghan said.

Alden could hardly breathe. The palms of her hands were clammy and cold.

Artie Rosenberg moved to the edge of the stage. The excited chatter in the theatre broke off as he introduced himself to the group.

"I'm Artie, and in case you haven't met her yet, this is Clare Proctor, development director of the Pantages."

Clare greeted the auditioning performers. "I've got some great news. The master of ceremonies for our vaudeville show is going to be my brother, Keller Grant."

"Keller Grant? The actor?" gasped someone in the audience.

"He'll be joining us a couple of days before the show," Clare continued. Spontaneous applause rose from the crowd.

"*The* Keller Grant? I can't believe it!" exclaimed another woman who held on to several Hula-Hoops and two small dogs.

"Keller Grant's so funny. I loved his last movie," gushed a theatre-camp kid Alden didn't know.

"Alden, you never told us Keller Grant was your uncle," chided Jenna.

"Okay. Now it's audition time!" said Artie. The crowd's enthusiasm turned to hushed, nervous whispers. "I know tryouts can be tough, but you need to remember that I'm on your side. Just show me what you can do. Plus," he said, smiling, "we want to reopen the Pantages with the best entertainment this theatre has seen since the great days of vaudeville! So give it all you've got."

The auditioners let out loud, enthusiastic shouts and whoops. Alden sat up straighter, feeling a rush of adrenaline.

Her mother flipped through the stack of audition forms in her hand. "We've divided your auditions into categories. Magicians in one group, comedians in another, and singers and dancers into other groups. Anyone wishing to audition for the chorus can go upstairs to the grand ballroom with our choreographer, Jill Hyatt." Alden's mother looked around. "Jill?" A perky redhead jumped up from her seat and waved. "Jill's from the dance department at the university. She's going to be teaching you a dance routine that we'll use for the opening of the show."

"Anyone wanting to dance in the chorus, come with me!" Jill said.

"That's me," said Jenna, grabbing her dance bag.

Potential dancers, including Josh Henderson, followed Jill up the aisle.

"I hope Jenna gets in," Meghan said. "She's a great dancer, just not very confident."

Artie Rosenberg was speaking to the rest of the group again. "We're going to start with the singers, then the comedians, and then the dance acts. After lunch, we'll come back and audition magicians, acrobats, and novelty acts. Okay? Let's get started!"

The auditions began. Singer after singer belted out songs. Some sang well, while others fell apart. Through it all, Artie Rosenberg was polite and professional. Theatre-camp kid Garrett Ramsey crooned a Ray Bolger tune, and Meghan Friedman sang an old music hall song.

Then Melody Reynolds's name was called. Alden watched as she confidently walked up the alcove stairs and onto the stage, handed her music to the accompanist, and turned toward the audience. Alden envied her composure.

Melody began to sing. Her voice was rich and smoky, her face lost in the lyrics. Melody reached the climax of the song, her voice soaring passionately, resonating throughout the theatre. The accompanist played the last note, and the theatre was silent.

Alden realized she was holding her breath. The Friedman twins had been right. Melody's talent was marvelous. The Pantages vaudeville show would be lucky to have her as a headliner.

Artie moved on to the comedians. Alden had a little time before they started auditioning the dance routines, so she apprehensively snuck though the alcove and up the steps to the backstage area. Walter was sitting at the stage manager's desk in semidarkness, the spot lit only by the spill of lights from the stage.

"Hi."

"Hey, kid. How ya doing?"

"Nervous."

"Don't be. Use the energy of the Pantages."

"What's that?"

"You'll see once you get out there." He smiled at her. "Melody Reynolds is quite a singer."

"Yeah," Alden said. "She's got one of the best voices I've ever heard."

Walter and Alden watched from the wings as the comedians performed their stand-up acts.

"Where's Raccoon?"

"He's coming later. I thought his being here would make me more jittery than I already am."

"And now?"

"I wish he was here," Alden confessed.

"Well, you'd better get your shoes on," Walter said. "The dance group is next, and you're up second."

Alden's stomach churned as she stumbled back down the steps and through the alcove to her seat. She grabbed her shoes and music, trying to swallow. But her mouth was like cotton, and her knees started to quiver. "Pull yourself together!" she told herself. "You have to nail this! You have to do well, for Julie's sake."

Alden moved back into the alcove, out of sight of the audience, and took a deep breath. She sank down onto the steps and shakily pulled on her tap shoes. Then she heard a popping sound, and Julie walked through the wall.

"Julie! What are you doing here? You could be discovered!"

"Nah. We're out of sight. I couldn't let you audition without seeing you first."

"Thanks, but...you'd better make it quick."

"Are you okay?"

"Nervous." Julie hugged her tightly and whispered into her ear, "You can do this, Allie. You're really good. I'll be in the balcony watching."

"But what if someone sees you up—"

"No one will be looking at the balcony. They'll be watching you."

"Julie, you can't take the chance of being exposed!"

Julie ignored her. "I also wanted to give you this." She opened Alden's hand and pressed something into her palm. "My mother gave it to me when I was little. I had it on the day I died. I want you to have it."

Alden heard someone approaching the alcove. "Someone's coming!" she whispered frantically.

With a sharp crack, Julie disappeared through the wall.

"Who ya talking to?" Taylor stood in the entrance to the alcove, watching her sharply.

"What? Oh...uh, I was just...talking to myself. You know...nerves before my audition." Had he heard Alden talking to Julie? Had he seen her walk through the wall?

Taylor looked suspiciously around the alcove. "Did you know this theatre has a secret?"

Alden eyed him warily. "No."

"It's haunted."

"That's ridiculous," Alden scoffed, perhaps a bit too loudly.

"That's right, haunted—by ghosts."

"There's no such thing as ghosts," Alden said hotly. "And don't start rumors. We don't want anything getting out about the theatre being haunted. It could hurt the show."

Taylor stepped out of the alcove and looked up at the balcony. "A girl fell from up there, fell to her death. She could be a ghost now, a ghost who lives here."

Alden panicked. Her audition was next, and Julie was going to watch her from the balcony. She had to keep Taylor from looking up there! She had to do something!

"You're trying to scare me and take my mind off my audition." Alden put her hand on Taylor's chest, slowly pushing him back into the alcove. "That's really sweet of you." Alden moved closer to him. "I'm going to watch your audition," she whispered. "I bet you make it."

"Are you kidding? I'll make it."

"Aren't you nervous?"

"Nope. I don't get scared."

"I'm up soon, and I've got butterflies."

He ran his finger down the side of her cheek. "Alden…"

"I'm next. Be sure to watch me."

Alden grabbed her music and ran up the stairs into the darkened wings, repulsed by her flirtation. Well, it had been for a good cause. She leaned against the fly rail. Taylor thought the Pantages was haunted. He knew someone had died in the theatre! She had been stupid to think that no one else in Smithfield knew. Even though Juliette's death had been a long time ago, it must be common knowledge among longtime Smithfield residents.

Julie's present was still clasped tightly in Alden's fist. She'd forgotten all about it. Opening her palm, she sighed with delight. It was a small cameo pin—a ballerina carved in creamy ivory was dancing on a rose-colored background. She turned it over. The gold backing was engraved with the words, *To my loving daughter.*

"It's beautiful," Alden breathed. This pin might be the only thing from her past that went with Julie when she crossed over into the ghost world. She had placed it in Alden's hand so lovingly and had taken such a chance giving it to her. She curved her fingers around the beautiful gift. It was Julie's prized keepsake, and she'd given it to Alden! Her knees were no longer shaking.

"Alden Proctor," Artie Rosenberg's voice called from the house.

"Alden!" whispered Walter. "You're on!"

Calmly, Alden walked through the wings, stepped onto the brightly lit stage, and handed her music to the accompanist. Then she crossed to the center and looked up. As promised, Julie was standing in the balcony, her hands clenched together under her chin. The music started, and Alden began.

Afterward, Alden didn't remember the audition. With Julie's pin clutched tightly in her hand, she forgot the people watching in the audience and let her dancing carry her up to where Julie stood, cheering her on. Walter had been right. She had felt an energy pulsating through her as she moved. Then, before she knew it, it was over. Alden looked up to the balcony. Julie gave her a victory thumbs-up and then walked through the wall. She was safe, for now. Alden walked off the stage and into the wings.

"Fantastic, Alden," said Walter, clapping her on the back.

Out in the house, Artie Rosenberg said, "Clare, you didn't tell me your daughter was a hoofer."

"I'm as surprised as you are."

"She needs a little work on selling it, but I think we can get her there. Let's finish up the last few dance auditions and get some lunch."

Alden crossed through the alcove and into the house. Taylor was leaning against the wall, facing the stage.

"Did you watch me?" she asked.

"I did."

Good. Then he probably didn't see Julie in the balcony.

"Not too shabby, Alden." He moved closer to her. "I'm not on until after lunch. What were we talking about before your audition?"

"I forget," Alden said dismissively. "I…I've gotta go. See ya."

"Hey, wait a minute…"

But Alden grabbed her dance bag from the seat, ran up the aisle, and out the theatre entrance, racing for home.

The rest of that day and what remained of the weekend were an anxious waiting game. Had she made it? How would Julie feel if she hadn't? Would she forgive her? Finally, after school the following Monday, Alden joined a loud and anxious group of theatre kids in the lobby of the theatre. The cast list would be posted today.

"Oh, I hope I made it! So many people auditioned. Jill Hyatt rocks!"

Alden's mom came down the stairs and greeted the chattering group. "The cast list has been posted on the call-board by the stage door."

Everyone raced backstage. Alden hung back.

"Alden, aren't you going to look?"

"I dunno. Maybe I'll wait till everyone's gone."

Her mom looked at Alden, her eyes misty.

"I'm proud of you, Alden. I wish my father could have seen your audition."

"I miss him."

"I know you do, honey. So do I."

"Mom...do you think Grandpa would have thought..." Alden gulped. The tears were coming. "Would he have thought I was any good?"

"I know he would have. Artie Rosenberg did."

Alden blinked the tears clear and looked at her mother with surprise. "Really?"

"I couldn't say anything to you before today. Why don't you go see?"

Was it possible? Was her mother implying that she'd made the show?

"Did *you* have anything to do with the casting?"

"No. Artie made all the decisions."

Slowly, Alden walked toward the black-and-gold theatre doors.

"Mom?"

"Yeah?"

Alden ran back and hugged her. "Thank you. Thanks for bringing us to Smithfield...and to the Pantages."

Her mom gruffly cleared her throat and lovingly pushed Alden away. "Go on. Go look at the list."

Alden ran down the aisle, up the stairs, and into the back hallway. A small crowd was still gathered around the call-board. Several girls were sniffling; others looked dazed. Garrett was pumping his fist in the air.

Jenna saw her first. "Alden, come look. I made it! I made the dancing chorus!"

"I made the show too," said Meghan. "Not as a soloist, but I'm in the chorus."

Alden reached the call-board. The others moved out of her way so she could stand directly in front of it. At the top was a note from Artie Rosenberg thanking everyone for auditioning and announcing the first rehearsal date. Alden skimmed through it quickly, and then her eyes found the cast list.

HEADLINERS
Sean Silvers and Mary Carol—George Burns
and Gracie Allen skit
Lloyd Van Sweden—Juggler
Melody Reynolds—Singer
Claudia Stroly—Trained Poodles
Taylor McCord—Magician
Sarah Maria Albertonio—Opera Singer

Melody was a headliner. So was Taylor McCord. Next, the cast listed the singers and dancers. The Friedman twins, Garrett, Josh, and many other theatre-camp kids had made the chorus.

Then she saw her own name.

FILLER ACTS
Bradley and Casey Fifer—"Who's on First" Abbott
and Costello routine
Alden Proctor—Tap Dance routine
Nic and Brooke Stevens, TJ and Liz Rubin—The Four Cohans

She'd made it! She wasn't a headliner, but her dance routine would be a filler act, and she was also listed in the chorus. Alden could picture her grandfather's proud face. She'd done it! Stunned, she turned from the call-board.

Melody was watching her closely. "Congratulations."

"Oh. Ah…thanks."

"You're a pretty good tapper. Didn't you just start taking lessons?"

"Yeah."

"Then I guess you're a natural. You've earned my respect."

Melody was revealing a sense of fairness Alden hadn't seen before. Was she offering an olive branch of friendship? Not sure if she could trust her, Alden was silent. Melody eyes fell to the floor. She moved away from Alden and started down the hallway.

"Melody, wait." Alden ran and caught up to her. "You've got one of the best voices I've ever heard. I knew you'd be cast as a headliner."

Melody hesitated. "But you've heard Broadway singers."

"You're just as good. Really."

Melody gave her a brilliant smile. "Thanks, Alden."

"Hey, you guys," said Garrett. "Wanna go pick up our scripts? They're in the office upstairs."

"I'll be up in a minute," Alden said.

Melody turned to Alden. "See you at rehearsal?"

"Yes. See ya, Melody."

Now Alden was alone in the hallway. She glanced at the cast list again and was hardly able to control her feet as they started tapping on the concrete. She had to find Julie! She ran up the stairs, flew down the hallway, and burst into the last dressing room.

"Julie?" There she was, sitting on the makeup counter. "Julie, I got in! I made the vaudeville show."

Julie threw her arms around Alden and hugged her tight. "I knew you'd make it! As soon as I saw your audition, I knew. You were wonderful...and you did it for me."

"I did it so you can take my place and dance in front of Alives instead of ghosts. But I couldn't have done it without you—or without this."

Alden held out Julie's cameo pin. "It's beautiful. I know it brought me luck. But I can't keep it."

"I want you to have it."

"Your mother gave it to you."

"You're the best friend I've ever had, Alden. My mother would have wanted me to give it to you."

"Then I'll treasure it forever."

"The news is spreading about the Pantages rejoining the ghost circuit," Julie said. "Every ghost act will either perform in our show or be in the audience. Kean's going to have a hard time deciding which acts to schedule, whom to feature, and who'll headline. Don't forget, you're invited to our dress rehearsal."

"Imagine, the ghost vaudeville show performing here—and on the same night as ours! I wish my grandfather could have seen it."

"Did you ever stop and wonder if your grandfather died completely?" Julie asked.

"What do you mean?"

"Maybe he's a theatre ghost."

13

There is something in the wind.

—William Shakespeare, The Comedy of Errors

Alden woke to warm April sun streaming through her window. She lay on her back, blinking her eyes, relishing the bright daylight. It was Saturday and the first day of rehearsal. Today they were starting choreography. Alden worried about keeping up with the other dancers, but as she threw off her covers, she vowed to try.

For the first time in many months, Alden pulled her bike out of the garage and rode to the theatre. The breeze smelled of spring and rustled her hair. Alden entered the stage door and, throwing her dance bag over her shoulder, ran up the stairs, calling Julie's name.

"In here."

Alden ran down the hall and then stopped short. The dressing room had been turned into a sewing room. Bolts of fabric were stacked on the makeup tables, and boxes overflowed with ribbon and trim. Julie was seated at an antique sewing machine.

"Does that thing even work?"

"Of course, silly," Julie replied. "I've almost finished our second costume."

Alden picked up one of two identical white felt hats with peach ribbon tied around the brim. She knew from one of her many conversations with Walter that it was called a cloche, a popular style from the 1920s.

"Done." Julie pushed her chair back from the sewing machine and stood up. "This one's yours, and mine's hanging up over there." She held it up next to Alden's body. The dress was pale-yellow silk with peach flowers and decorated with cream-colored lace and ribbon, similar to the dresses that Gloria and Irene wore. Julie watched Alden anxiously.

"You made this?"

"Sure," Julie said proudly.

"It's beautiful. I didn't know you could sew." Eagerly, Alden put on the dress. The soft fabric flowed perfectly over her shoulders and hips. "It fits! How did you…"

"We're the same size, silly!" Julie said as she pulled on her own dress.

Alden and Julie added stockings, gloves, tap shoes, and then the hats. Standing side by side, they peered into the dressing-room mirror.

"I don't believe it! You can hardly tell us apart!" Alden said.

"I told you my plan would work."

"Julie…what exactly *is* the plan?"

"I *have* one!" Julie said defensively.

"Well, I think you need to tell me. Rehearsals are starting today. There's only three weeks until the show."

"First, I made these identical costumes in case something goes wrong."

Alden began to feel uneasy. "What do you mean, Julie? What could go wrong?"

Julie ignored her. "Your final dress rehearsal is our first test. If we get away with it then, the performance will be a piece of cake!"

"How? Exactly *how* are we going to pull this off?"

"Okay, okay. Just before it's your turn to perform, you'll slip into the alcove. I'll come through the wall, run up the stairs, and walk onto the stage. Once the number's over, I'll meet you in the alcove and disappear through the wall again."

"What if—"

"It'll work. Trust me."

"I hope you're right." Nervously, Alden smoothed her new costume.

"Thanks again for doing this for me," Julie said. "It means a lot to me."

"Sure," responded Alden with a confidence she didn't feel. Still, Julie's plan wasn't bad. They did look alike in the costumes, and the hats covered most of their faces. It actually might work.

"I gotta get going."

Hurriedly, she pulled off the costume and reached for her dance clothes. Alden ran through the theatre and up to the ballroom. Apprehensively, she stared at the dancers filling the room. Jill Hyatt, the show's choreographer, was warming up in the corner. Melody, Josh, Garrett, and several other dancers Alden didn't know were stretching on the other side of the room.

Jenna greeted her. "You ready for this?"

"I didn't realize they were putting everyone into the dance numbers. I hope I can keep up."

"No worries," Jenna reassured her.

Meghan dropped her bag next to Alden's. "Nice dance clothes."

"Oh yeah...my mom." Alden self-consciously looked down at her stomach and thighs. Almost a year ago, they would have been bulging, showing every large roll on her body. Now, her muscles were firm and toned. Her plumpness had been replaced with a tall leanness.

Over the next three hours, Jill taught them the choreography for the opening and closing numbers. Her direction was calm and encouraging. Some of the steps were tricky, but Alden managed to stay with everyone. By the end of the morning, she didn't want to stop.

"Thanks, everybody," Jill said. "Take a lunch break, and then we'll get back at it."

"That was fantastic," Alden said to the twins.

"Hey, Garrett," said Meghan. "Where's Taylor?"

"I'm clueless."

"He couldn't make rehearsal today," Melody said. "Something about a newspaper interview."

"Are they doing a story about magicians?" asked Garrett.

"No, something about the theatre being haunted."

"What?" screamed the twins in unison.

"No way," said Josh.

"He said somebody died in the Pantages a long time ago and haunts the theatre."

"For real?" asked Meghan.

Alden gnawed the inside of her cheek.

"I've heard some creepy stories about the theatre, too," said Melody. "Taylor's determined to find out."

"Is he going ghost hunting?" teased Garrett.

"Do you think the ghost could be watching us right now?" Jenna asked nervously.

"Watching *you*, Jenna," Meghan joked, grabbing her sister. Jenna squeaked, and everyone laughed—except Alden.

"Anyway, ghost or no ghost, I'm starving," said Garrett. "Let's get some lunch."

Alden hung back. "I…uh, I'll meet you guys back here after lunch. I'm gonna find Walter."

The group headed down the stairs, their voice chorusing, "The Pantages—haunted? Wouldn't that be cool?"

"I'd love to see a ghost."

"Me too!"

Rattled, Alden stood alone in the ballroom. She needed to see Julie. She needed to warn her about Taylor's ghost hunt.

"Julie?"

Moments later there was a familiar popping sound and a loud crack, and then Julie walked through the ballroom wall. "How was rehearsal?"

"Good. Listen, Julie, there's this kid in the show who's going around telling everybody the Pantages is haunted."

"It is!" Julie laughed.

"Julie, this is serious. I think he might have heard us talking in the alcove on audition day! He also knows that someone died in the theatre."

"But he doesn't know it was me."

"I don't trust him. There's something about him…he's a little off."

"You're still gonna go through with our plan, aren't you, Alden?"

"Of course! But, Julie, you *have* to be careful."

"I will."

"Promise me!" Alden demanded. "He's the type of Alive who'd expose you."

"Nothing to worry about."

Alden wasn't so sure.

14

It was a long and gloomy night that gathered on me, haunted by the ghosts of many hopes, of many dear remembrances, many errors, many unavailing sorrows and regrets.

—Charles Dickens, David Copperfield

Alden couldn't concentrate. She doodled on her vocabulary assignment in school, uncertainty plaguing her. Julie's plan to dance in her place might work, but would they pull it off? And why did Taylor want everyone to know the Pantages was haunted?

Finally, after debate club finished, Alden grabbed her backpack and ran as quickly as she could to the Pantages theatre. Eagerly, she rounded the corner of Main Street and then stopped short. Two police cars were parked on the sidewalk and blocking the theatre alley, their red lights whirling. Alden ran toward the theatre, skirting around the police cars. Camp students huddled together in small groups, hugging each other and crying. When they saw Alden, they wouldn't meet her eyes. They just whispered to each other and scuffed their shoes on the pavement.

Jenna and Meghan were standing next to the stage door, their eyes red rimmed. "Alden, I don't think you should go in there," warned Meghan, grabbing her arm.

Alden shook her off and pushed through the door. Two policemen were standing outside the archive room, speaking to Walter.

"Walter! Where's my mom?" Her voice cracked. She was barely able to get the words out.

"Your mom's fine," he said, grabbing her shoulders. Alden felt her knees buckle. Relief flooded through her. "She's upstairs in the dressing rooms with the police detective. They're taking pictures for evidence." Alden brushed past Walter.

"Ah…miss," said a police officer, stepping in front of her. "Crime scene."

Alden looked past the policeman and into the archive room. It was unrecognizable. Filing cabinets were turned on their side, their contents littering the floor. The desk was overturned, its drawers hanging upside down. The framed pictures she and Walter had so lovingly chosen for the lobby display were smashed. Broken glass lay everywhere.

Scrawled across the far wall in garish red paint were the words, "Proctors Go Home. Vaudeville is DEAD."

Alden looked at the written threats with horror. She squeezed her eyes tight, and angry tears spilled from their corners. "Who did this? Who could have done this?"

Walter put a comforting hand on her shoulder. "We don't know, Alden. The police will investigate. We'll try to find out. We—"

Alden jerked away from him and appealed to the police officer. "Can I go find my mom?"

The officer nodded empathetically. "Just don't touch anything."

Alden walked out onto the stage. Lighting instruments were broken into pieces and strewn around the wings. Red paint was splashed on the fly rail and the stage manager's podium. The beautiful main curtain Walter had taught Alden to fly the first time she'd visited the Pantages hung in ragged shreds.

Alden was both terrified and furious. Who could hate the Pantages this much? Feeling as if she was going to vomit, Alden dragged herself up the stairs and stumbled into the first dressing room, where she found evidence of more violence. The mirrors were shattered, and the lightbulbs that normally surrounded them were smashed. More graffiti covered the walls. "Go back to New York. Burn the Pantages."

Repulsed, Alden threw her back against the wall and sank to the floor. "Why? Why would someone do this?" She clenched her fists and pounded them on her thighs. Then she looked up to see her mother out in the hall with the police detective.

"That's it for now, Mrs. Proctor. Here's a copy of the police report for the insurance company. There's no evidence of a forced entry, so it might be an inside job. Do you have any employees who would have a reason to do this?"

"No one," Clare murmured.

"An inside job?" Alden thought. "What are the police implying?"

"We'll try to get to the bottom of it."

"Thank you," her mother said as the detective left.

"Mom?"

Her mother turned, her face contorted with pain and worry.

"Oh Alden." Alden ran into her mother's arms. "I'm sorry, baby, I'm so sorry."

Alden cried into her shoulder, sob after sob, until she eventually hic-cupped out, "I don't understand."

"I don't either, honey. Obviously someone doesn't want us here."

"Mom, it says 'Proctors go home.'"

"I don't want you to worry, Alden. The police will handle it. I called Greg. Glenco is putting a guard outside our house and at the theatre."

"We need a guard?"

"They say it's just a precaution. I'm sure the insurance will cover the damage. I just don't know how soon things can be repaired." Watching her daughter closely, she said, "Alden, I'm not sure we can continue with the vaudeville show."

"No, Mom, no!"

"But, sweetie, I don't see how I can get everything fixed and have the theatre ready in time. There's too much damage."

"Mom, Mayor Klein and the city council said that if the vaudeville show's a success, they'd forget about Brennan's offer to buy the theatre. If we don't do the show, we could lose the Pantages!"

"I know. I just..." Her mother's voice cracked. She was trying to be brave, but Alden could see that her mom was as shaken as she was.

There had to be a way. "Mom, could you do me a favor? Ask Walter to gather all the theatre kids in the front lobby. I'll be there in a little bit. I just need a minute."

"I don't think I should leave you alone."

"I'm okay. Really."

Numbly, her mother nodded and left. Once she was out of sight, Alden ran to the last dressing room.

"Julie? Julie!" Alden paced back and forth. There was no evidence of a break-in. Was it possible? Could the damage to the theatre have been done by a ghost? "Come on, Julie, I need you!"

The popping sound began, and then Julie walked through the wall.

"Julie, have you seen it? Have you seen what someone did?"

"Yes. Red thinks it happened late last night."

"The police said it could be an inside job."

"I—"

"Julie, could this have been done by a ghost?"

"There's a possibility…"

"What possibility?"

"There's another ghost who lives here. I've never seen him. He was already in hiding when I became a ghost. Red, who's lived here the longest, hasn't seen him for a long, long time."

"The first time I met your aunts, Irene mentioned there was another ghost. But why would he do this? I thought everyone loved the Pantages."

"Everyone except this ghost. He hates the theatre."

"Why?"

"Because he's Mr. Pantages's son. Only old Mr. Pantages never acknowledged that fact."

"But why would he threaten my mother and me?"

"I don't know, Alden. I just don't know. Red's gone to New York to tell Kean what happened. Maybe they'll know what to do."

"Can Red stop him from doing something like this again?"

"He could…if they battle. But ghost battles often don't end well. If their astral charges collide, they could obliterate each other."

"They wouldn't exist as ghosts anymore?"

"They would disappear forever. It happened about fifty years ago between two ghosts who'd been feuding actors when they were alive. Kean wasn't able to stop them before they destroyed each other."

Worried about her ghost friends, Alden left the dressing room only after Julie promised to let her know as soon as Red returned.

The immediate problem was the show. If the vaudeville show wasn't a success, and Brennan tore the theatre down, Julie and the others would lose their home. The show had to happen—for Julie and the theatre ghosts' survival as well as for the Pantages. Alden had asked her mom to have Walter call together all the theatre-camp students. Now, walking up the aisle toward the lobby, Alden didn't know what to say to them. What had compelled her to call a meeting?

Alden pushed through the theatre doors into the lobby to a cacophony of anxious voices.

"I don't know if my father will let me come back here again. He's on his way here to pick me up."

"Did you see what was written on the walls? Someone has it in for the Proctors!"

"Does this mean there won't be a show?"

"No show? Are they canceling the show?"

Alden raised her voice above the din. "Of course there's going to be a show."

All eyes turned toward her, and the crowd quieted down. Her eyes darted over the group, focusing briefly on the Friedman twins and Garrett and then on Melody and Josh. They stared back. Alden knew they were anxious, waiting for their fears to be calmed, all wanting answers. She cleared her throat. The silence in the lobby lengthened. The kids rustled their feet and began murmuring to each other. Alden was losing them, failing the Pantages. Her eyes settled on Walter, who was standing on the staircase behind the others. Her shoulders sagged helplessly.

"Use the energy of the Pantages," he mouthed.

The energy of the Pantages. The energy of the Pantages. She wasn't sure what that was, but deep inside, she knew it existed. Julie had it. Alden had used it during her audition. While she was dancing, she had felt a rush, a surge of power, unaware of where it had come from. Now, as Alden looked at the theatre kids standing in front of her, she thought about the hundreds of people who had performed at the Pantages for over a century and the thousands of audience members who had applauded and laughed. She wasn't about to let that history disappear. She gave Walter a determined nod.

"The vaudeville show will still happen as scheduled." Sighs of relief were audible from the crowd. Alden's voice got stronger. "But my mother and I can't do it alone. There just isn't time. We need your help. All of you."

A few of the camp kids nodded their heads. Most stared at her with blank faces.

Meghan piped up. "But what can we do, Alden?"

Alden couldn't answer. Her mouth felt dry. She didn't have a plan. She'd foolishly gathered everyone together without a clue what to do.

Jenna stepped forward and clasped Alden's hand. "We can all get to work, that's what we can do."

Alden squeezed Jenna's fingers gratefully. "That's right." Alden searched the crowd. "Garrett, your parents own a hardware store. Can you get them to donate paint, just until the insurance check arrives?" She held her breath, hoping Garrett would agree.

"If my parents wanna see me on stage, they'd better."

Everyone laughed, the tension already easing. Garrett moved next to Jenna and grabbed her hand. Jenna's face blushed pink.

Melody said, "I'll get my parents to donate new mirrors and lightbulbs."

"My dad's an electrician," offered Josh. "Maybe he can repair the lighting instruments."

The kids were all making suggestions now, confidence coming back into their voices.

"Okay," said Alden. "This Saturday is theatre-cleanup day. Bring everything you can and any additional help you can find. We're taking the Pantages back from whoever did this! The vaudeville show will go on."

A cheer went up as the theatre kids made their way out the lobby doors.

Her mom had joined Walter on the staircase. Her face was proud.

"It's gonna happen, Mom. We're gonna get through this." Adrenalin pumped through Alden.

Or was it the energy of the Pantages?

15

Coming together is a beginning.
Keeping together is progress.
Working together is success.

—HENRY FORD

On Saturday morning, Alden and Raccoon hurried downtown, both lost in thought. After the Pantages had been vandalized, Raccoon had pumped Alden with questions, and she'd tearfully explained to him what had happened to the theatre. When she'd told him about the graffiti, Raccoon's face had grown stormy.

"I hope they catch the thugs who did this."

"Me too," she said, wondering how easy it would be to catch an angry theatre ghost.

Raccoon walked into the archive room and stared at the graffiti in disbelief.

His jaw tight, he immediately grabbed a filing cabinet and righted it.

The stage door opened to the chatter of helpers. Meghan and Jenna, Melody, Josh, and Garrett made their way into the wings. Tagging along behind them was Taylor McCord. Alden was surprised to see him.

"This is my friend Raccoon, and you all know Walter." Alden watched Melody as she made the introduction. She was studying Raccoon, her green eyes carefully appraising him. Alden's chest felt tight. She knew Raccoon wasn't exclusively *her* friend. So why was she suddenly feeling so possessive? Alden forced herself to focus on the cleanup.

More theatre kids arrived, many with their parents, carrying gallons of paint, rollers, and ladders. A man with curly black hair pushed a hand truck with large boxes on it down the hallway.

"The dressing rooms are upstairs, Dad," said Melody. Then she turned to Alden. "My dad's in retail. These are unused mirrors from the department store."

"I'm grateful, Melody."

They set to work. The new mirrors were hung and lightbulbs replaced. Fresh paint covered the graffiti on the walls. Josh's father and other parents repaired the lights. Her mom ordered a new main curtain, specifying a rush delivery.

While they worked, Alden wondered when Red would be back. The guard stationed in the alley provided reassurance to everyone but her. Only Alden knew that the culprit was possibly a ghost lurking somewhere within the theatre walls. She felt a little more secure with Raccoon there.

Toward the end of the day, Walter asked Alden and Raccoon to go to the prop room and gather canes for a dance number that would open the second act. Alden and Raccoon obediently descended to the basement level. PROP ROOM was written on the first door.

"Think there's any damage in here?" Raccoon asked, trying to open the door. "It's stuck. I guess the wood's swollen." He shouldered it and forced it open. The bulb in the cage on the ceiling had burned out; the only light in the room filtered in from the open doorway.

Squinting, Alden said, "Look at all this stuff! I never knew what was in here before today." The small room was filled with chairs, chaise lounges, desks, and tables. Shelves overflowed with lamps, candelabra, baskets, lanterns, and bowls. Boxes stored wooden apples and grapes; vases held fabric flowers. There were wooden barrels and sawhorses, saddles, and lasso ropes. Round metal bins held pitchforks, brooms, swords, wooden rifles, and shepherd's crooks. Everything was filthy.

"Looks like this room survived the graffiti but not fifty years of dust," Raccoon remarked.

"I don't think even Walter knew all this stuff was here," Alden replied as she worked her way through the maze of props to a stack of cardboard boxes. "I wonder what's in these."

Raccoon moved directly behind her. She could feel his breath on the back of her neck and the warmth of his body. Uncertainly, Alden shifted closer to the stack of boxes and pulled one open. Raccoon leaned over her shoulder, resting his hand on her waist, his chest touching her back. A jolt ran through her at his touch.

Neatly laid inside the boxes and sprinkled with cedar chips were dozens of costumes wrapped in brown paper.

"Maybe these could be used in the vaudeville show," Raccoon suggested softly.

Alden could barely answer. The nearness of Raccoon in the darkened room created an unfamiliar ache.

"I think so," she replied. Their relationship had changed since Alden had first met Raccoon. They were closer and trusted each other now, but this was the closest they had come to any physical contact. She had trouble admitting it to herself—but she liked it. It felt right. But did he feel the same way?

Raccoon stepped around her, lifted the box of costumes off the stack, and opened another one. Alden immediately missed the warmth and closeness of his body touching hers. What had just happened? Had Raccoon leaned against her to see the contents of the boxes, or was it something else? Had she imagined the closeness? Confused by the jumping butterflies in her stomach, she pulled a costume from the box.

"What are you doing?" Taylor asked, interrupting her jumble of emotions. He stood in the doorway, with Melody behind him. Alden wondered how long they'd been standing there. Taylor was staring at her, his eyes steely.

"They're costumes," Raccoon answered, bristling. Alden was unsure why he seemed so annoyed.

"We came to tell you guys that there are cookies and lemonade for everyone," Melody said. "And, Alden, we've got something to show you."

"Sure." With an excuse to get out of the dark prop room and temporarily leave her uncertainty behind, Alden brushed past Taylor and escaped with Melody up the stairs.

"So, are you and Raccoon hooked up?" Melody asked.

"What do you mean?"

"It seemed like you two were pretty cozy in there."

"We're just friends." But as soon as Alden said it, she knew that she wished otherwise. She wanted to be more than friends with Raccoon. Alden was now in unexpected territory. "Why do you ask?"

"Taylor didn't seem too happy, that's all. You know he has a thing for you, right?"

"What?"

"Never mind. Come on, I want you to see the theatre."

As Melody led her onto the stage, Raccoon and Taylor caught up with them. Theatre kids, parents, and volunteers stood to one side of the stage, all watching Alden. The stage floor sported a new coat of black paint, the lighting instruments had been rehung on the batons, and the destroyed main curtain had been taken down.

"The dressing rooms and the archive room are back to normal, too," Melody said.

Alden was unable to speak.

Clare moved out of the group to stand alongside Alden and address the volunteers. "We can't thank you enough."

"We did it, Alden!" Jenna said.

Garrett stepped forward and slapped Alden on the back. "Thanks for making us a part of the solution. Now we can start rehearsal."

Everyone was watching Alden, waiting for her response. The theatre cleanup had worked. The vaudeville show was going to happen.

"The show must go on!" Alden joyfully yelled.

Josh and Garrett whooped, and everyone cheered, while her mom and Gina served cookies.

"Alden?" Raccoon called, pulling her away from the group. Alden tensed. Did her tangled emotions show on her face?

"Are you okay with me working backstage for the vaudeville show? Walter asked me."

Alden looked into his bright, blue eyes. "It's…it's great."

Raccoon stepped closer to her. "I was hoping you'd say that, 'cause I wouldn't do it unless you wanted me to. You were right. I should have come to meet everyone sooner. But now that I have, I like it here." His eyes searched hers, waiting for approval. Alden's mind was back in the prop room with Raccoon's hand on her waist, his breath on her hair. "You okay?"

"I...um..." Blood rushed to her face. Had he guessed she was think-ing about him? "I'm fine." It came out more coldly than she'd intended. Alden's eyes darted over to where Taylor leaned against the back wall. Raccoon followed her gaze, his face clouding over.

"I'm sorry, Raccoon. I'd love to have you work on the vaudeville show."

"Listen, in the prop room just now, did I *do* something?"

"I gotta go help my mom," Alden said abruptly.

Unaware either of Taylor's glare or Raccoon's confusion, Alden moved into the crowd of kids and grabbed a tray of cookies to pass out.

16

In the sweetness of friendship let there be laughter, for in the dew of little things the heart finds its morning and is refreshed.

—Kahlil Gibran

Alden had been avoiding Raccoon for a week. But now, riding her bike through Locust Park, she found herself looking for him. Of course, he wasn't there. She hadn't given him any reason to ride to the theatre with her. Ashamed, she pedaled harder. Plus, when she saw Raccoon at school, stupid excuses came out of her mouth. He seemed guarded and hurt, reverting to the Raccoon she'd known when they'd first met. Ever since the theatre-cleanup day, Alden was uncomfortable with what she now knew. She liked him—she liked him a lot. The realization had panicked her. She didn't want Raccoon to know, certain he didn't feel the same way about her. She'd convinced herself that what had happened in the prop room hadn't meant anything to him. She was a friend, and that was it. Alden couldn't talk about how she felt—even to Julie. Old insecurities were hard to shake.

When Alden walked into the archive room, Julie was waiting for her.

"Red's back. I told him how you got everyone to help repair the damage to the theatre."

"The other ghost...has Red seen him?"

"No. He never shows himself. We figured that you won." Then Julie quickly changed the subject. "Raccoon's out on the stage."

Alden swallowed and looked the other way. "He is?"

Julie studied her face. "He's been here all week, helping Walter paint the scenery. I've been helping with the props." Alden avoided Julie's eyes as she bent down to put on her dance shoes.

"Meet us when they break for lunch?" Julie insisted.

"I'll think about it." She gave Julie a weak smile. "I'd better get to rehearsal."

To avoid seeing Raccoon on the stage, Alden left through the stage door and ran around to the front of the theatre. "Coward," she scolded herself.

During the rehearsal, Alden's mind kept drifting to thoughts of Raccoon rather than concentrating on the dance steps. Jill Hyatt gave her a questioning look when she missed a section she'd previously nailed.

"Sorry," Alden apologized. Jill put the cast on break, and Alden grabbed her dance bag.

"Coming to lunch with us, Alden?" asked Jenna.

"Thanks, but I'm gonna eat lunch with Walter."

Jenna raised her eyebrows. "And Raccoon?"

"Whaddya mean?"

"Meghan and I ran into him a couple of days ago when we had our costume fittings. Isn't he helping with the show?"

"Yeah, he's...um...helping Walter paint the scenery."

Jenna snorted. "So that's why you're not going to lunch with us!"

"No, I..." Alden protested.

"It's okay, I understand," Jenna teased. "You've got better things to do than eat with us!" Jenna laughed as she bounced down the stairs. "He's hot, Alden! Go for it."

Alden walked into the back of the theatre and paused at the top of the aisle. An enormous canvas covered the entire width and depth of the stage. Raccoon was crouched down, mixing a bucket of paint. He wore the familiar muscle shirt and beat-up jeans with paint smears across his hips. His sandy-brown hair brushed his shoulders. He confidently measured different cans into the bucket before testing the color. Alden's throat was dry. She missed him. The last week had been stupid. If he didn't like her, she'd get over it. She'd rather be around him than not at all.

Julie appeared at her side. "He's not going to bite. You can do this." Julie linked her arm through Alden's and dragged her down the aisle.

"You know?"

"What are best friends for? Come on."

Alden jumped up onto the stage. "Hi."

Raccoon gave her a guarded look. "Hi back."

"Show me what you're doing."

Raccoon hesitated. Alden held her breath. Maybe she had blown it with him for good. Then he seemed to make a decision.

"Okay. First, Walter and I stretched this canvas out and stapled it down to the stage with bridges underneath it every few feet. The bridges are wooden structures that create an air gap between the floor and the drop." Raccoon picked up a small sketch. "This is the rendering with a grid drawn on it. We also put a larger grid on the canvas, and then we drew this exact picture onto the backdrop, and now we're painting it."

Alden moved closer to Raccoon to get a better view of the picture. "Show me."

Playfully, he pulled it out of her reach.

"Hey!"

He grinned devilishly, moving the drawing even farther away. Alden leaned over his arm.

"That's better," he whispered.

She elbowed him in the ribs. "Lemme see!"

Her hair fell on either side of her face, shielding her view of the painting. Raccoon reached over and gently pulled it back.

"Thanks," Alden breathed softly, meeting his eyes. Raccoon released her hair behind her shoulders. "Raccoon, listen…I'm sorry about this past week. I—"

"It's all right. Just don't shut me out again, okay?" His eyes were hopeful, pleading.

"I won't." Alden beamed at him. Could she have been wrong? Was there a possibility that he felt something for her?

"Look what the picture is, Allie!" Julie interrupted, jumping between them and grinning with pleasure as if she were responsible for their reconciliation. "Show her, Raccoon!" she insisted.

Raccoon was laughing. "Okay, okay, you crazy lady."

The picture was a depiction of New York's original theatre district with marquees crisscrossing at different angles to form an intricate connection of buildings, lights, and signs. Theatregoers were gazing up at the marquees with a sense of wonder.

"Look. That's Tony Pastor's vaudeville showplace," Julie said, pointing to one of the buildings, "and there's the Lyceum...and that's the George M. Cohan Theatre."

Alden smiled proudly at Raccoon. "It's wonderful."

"I'm not as good as Walter—yet. He's a great teacher, though. He went out to get us some sandwiches."

Julie skipped to the other side of the stage, admiring the backdrop.

"I missed you, Alden," Raccoon whispered softly. "You okay?"

He'd missed her!

"I'm good. It's all good."

Walter returned just then with the sandwiches, and they all sat on the edge of the stage, legs dangling into the pit, eating, and discussing the upcoming dress rehearsal.

When they'd finished their lunch, Walter said, "Okay, Raccoon, let's get back at it. We've gotta finish this backdrop."

Raccoon reluctantly stood up, not taking his eyes off Alden.

"I've gotta get back upstairs to rehearsal anyway," Alden said.

"Walk you home?" Raccoon asked.

"I'd like that."

17

They that dwell in the land of the shadow of death, upon them hath the light shined.

—*Isaiah 9:2*

The dogwood trees on Duke Street bloomed with white blossoms, and the westerly wind off the lake smelled sweet. Alden sat on the front porch, eating breakfast with Cleo and her mom. She closed her eyes and turned her face up to the sun.

Rehearsals were almost over. Uncle Keller would join the cast at tomorrow's final dress rehearsal. But as much as she was looking forward to the vaudeville show, Alden could think only about what would be happening *after* her rehearsal today. The ghosts were arriving! She was going to meet the vaudeville circuit ghosts!

Her mother interrupted her thoughts. "You ready for school?"

"Yeah, but I don't want to go. I wish I could just stay at the theatre."

"Well, there are a ton of things you could help me with. I'll tell you what," her mom said. "I'll let you take tomorrow off from school if you come help me at the theatre."

"Really?" The theatre instead of school? How cool was her mom?

Alden hadn't been sure how to ask for permission to stay after rehearsal today, because she couldn't let on what the real reason was. Maybe this was her chance. "Mom, if I don't have to get up for school tomorrow, can I stay late tonight and help Walter?"

"Okay, as long as you're home before dark."

Cleo took her cereal bowl from her. "Grab your backpack, kid. I'll run you over to school."

Alden stood up. "That's okay. It's such a beautiful morning, I think I'll walk."

Looking down the block, Cleo spied Raccoon walking toward the house. "Suit yourself," she teased.

That afternoon, during their last rehearsal in the ballroom, Jill had drilled the dancers over and over on the opening and closing numbers until their muscles had quivered with exhaustion. Alden didn't care. She knew the cast didn't mind either, since they were so pumped about the show. Alden said good-bye to the cast members and watched as they left through the lobby doors. When the last dancer had gone, Alden turned toward the theatre, hardly able to contain her excitement. Would the ghosts be in there? Quickly, she sprinted through the lobby, pausing at the black-and-gold doors to listen.

Everything was quiet. Alden pulled open the door and moved softly into the theatre. She recalled the first time she'd come to the Pantages. The quiet had been so eerie. Now, she loved the stillness.

The stage lights were ablaze, shining on Raccoon and Walter's new backdrop that now hung from a baton at the back of the stage. Looking at it, she was immediately swept back to New York City at the turn of the twentieth century.

"It's breathtaking," she whispered. Alden looked up at the domed ceiling, the balcony, and the theatre boxes. "It's really going to happen," she said. "The Pantages is going to reopen."

Grinning, she threw her dance bag onto a seat in the first row, ran up the alcove stairs, and onto the stage.

"Walter?" Her voice reverberated through the empty theatre. No response. The echo died away.

Alden crossed to the stage manager's podium and saw a folded piece of paper with her name on it.

Alden:

Raccoon and I left the stage lights on so you could see the finished backdrop. Before you leave, can you turn them off? Pull down the main lever on the lighting panel. The ghost light is rigged to turn on automatically. See you tomorrow night.

Thanks,
Walter

Alden stared at the lighting panel. If she turned off the stage lights, and the ghost light came on, what would happen? Would the ghosts arrive? Slowly, she walked to the panel, reached up, and pulled the main lever toward the floor. Instantly, the stage went dark, and only the ghost light illuminated the theatre. She released the lever, her hands shaking.

"Julie?" Her voice sounded unusually loud.

Alden waited, watching and listening. The theatre remained silent. Even Julie didn't seem to be around.

Disappointed, Alden made her way down the stairs, through the alcove, and into the house. She'd desperately wanted to see the ghost dress rehearsal. She wanted to meet performers who loved the theatre so much that they couldn't truly die. She wished she could see their reactions to the renovation of the Pantages—its past shabbiness transformed to its original grandeur.

Maybe Julie had been wrong. Maybe the ghosts hadn't chosen her. Alden knew how dangerous it was for ghosts to show themselves in human form to an Alive. Maybe they didn't trust her. Sadly, she grabbed her dance bag and started to leave through the house.

Then she heard a slow rumble, like faraway thunder, and felt a slight vibration that tickled her feet. Within seconds it increased. The rumble grew louder. The floor of the theatre was actually shaking! Frightened, Alden fell into a seat.

Pop. Pop. Pop. The now familiar sound of popping corn was coming from inside the walls. Pop, pop, pop. POP! POP! POP! It was happening so fast now that Alden couldn't distinguish the individual sounds. The popping became deafening. Alden wanted to cover her ears, but she didn't want to miss anything.

Crack! Suddenly, there was a commotion in the back hallway by the stage door, and Alden heard a man's demanding voice.

"Where's my dressing room? You know I need a massage before we begin rehearsal."

Crack! Ghosts walked through the walls and onto the stage.

Crack! Ghosts crashed through the outside theatre walls and into the aisles.

Crack! Ghosts ran down the spiral stairs.

At first there were twenty—and then thirty—and then forty more. With each crack, they were arriving, dusting themselves off and gazing around.

Alden sank lower into her seat and clutched her dance bag against her chest, watching with astonishment. They lugged suitcases, pushed steamer trunks, and carried boxes of props and costumes and musical instruments. A cacophony of yipping dogs clambered in the wings.

"Ah, the Pantages Theatre."

The voice was right behind her. Alden froze.

"It's about time they reopened this place."

"It was the best on the circuit."

"Looks like they've fixed it up a little."

Alden's teeth were chattering. She clenched her jaws, trying to stop them from banging together. She heard the same demanding voice again.

"Kean, my contract says my dressing room has to have a window! Does it have a window?"

A small blond man dressed in a well-tailored suit strode to center stage and looked around. His body was tight and compact. Following quickly behind him was an entourage of people pushing several hampers overflowing with ropes and pulleys. The loud-mouthed man was empty-handed.

"Did you get my fruit basket?"

Kean ran his hand through his hair. This condescending, strident man had to be George Templeton!

"Hi, Alden," Julie said, slipping into the seat next to her.

Alden tore her eyes away from the stage. "Julie! Where've you been? I didn't know what to do, where to go! Is it okay that I'm here?"

"Of course. You've been approved, and they're showing themselves."

"Are you sure?"

"They're in human form. If they hadn't chosen you, you wouldn't be able to see or hear anything. It'd just be an empty theatre."

Alden's eyes darted around, taking in as many of the ghost arrivals as she could.

Hundreds of ghosts had chosen her!

"Everyone's a little crazy right now," Julie said. "I love it."

The cracking continued as more and more ghosts walked through the walls. The balcony filled up, and the stage itself was bedlam.

"All right, everyone," Kean shouted over the clamor. "The show's lineup is posted on the call-board by the stage door. Headliners and filler acts—your dressing rooms are upstairs. Chorus singers, dancers, and musicians—downstairs in the rooms next to prop storage."

One-Armed Red walked onto the stage, calling loudly, "Half hour, folks. Half hour before the run-through."

Ghost actors grabbed suitcases and makeup cases and headed for the dressing rooms. Technicians ran up the spiral stairs to the catwalk.

Still astounded, Alden said to Julie, "Everyone here, all these people, are ghosts?"

"Yup. When they were alive, they loved the theatre and vaudeville, just like me. They couldn't bear to leave it." Julie grabbed her arm. "Look, over there."

Alden turned and saw a beautiful, dark-haired woman with translucent skin, huge almond eyes, and a pouty smile. She wore a green beaded dress with an elaborate headpiece. In her hand was a small blue glass bottle.

Alden gasped. "That's the Ziegfeld girl from the picture Walter found!"

"She's Olive Thomas, ghost of the New Amsterdam Theatre," whispered Julie. "You're right, Olive was a Follies girl. She was the toast of New York. Ziegfeld fancied her."

"What's the bottle for?"

"That's her pill bottle. She overdosed on medicine." Julie leaned closer to Alden and whispered, "Rumors said it was suicide."

Olive was surrounded by several attentive gentlemen in tuxedos. Alden watched as Olive flirtatiously patted the chest of one of her admirers.

"Alden, look! The theatre box!"

Alden whipped her head around. A tall man with windblown hair and wearing a clerical collar was greeting other ghosts and shaking their hands joyously.

"Is he a priest?"

"No." Julie laughed. "That's Mr. Belasco. He's a theatre owner and producer. They call him the Bishop of Broadway, 'cause he dresses like that. He still inhabits his theatre on Forty-Fourth Street. He hasn't left Broadway for eighty years, but since the Pantages is coming back to the circuit, he made the trip."

Alden sat up straighter. Now that Julie was next to her, she wasn't as frightened.

Ghosts continued to arrive through the theatre walls. Julie pointed to the stage. "That's Foster and Rascal over there, and next to the spiral staircase are Nelda Forester and Ida Murphy."

An enormous brown bear trotted onto the stage. Alden almost jumped out of her seat! "What the…"

Julie giggled. "That's Caroline, the dancing bear. Don't worry, she's really quite harmless."

The balcony was almost full. Members of the ghost audience were dressed in exquisite formal clothes. Alden recognized Ray Bolger, the scarecrow from *The Wizard of Oz*, and Harpo from the Marx Brothers movies she used to watch with Grandpa Charlie. The ghosts greeted one another with great enthusiasm.

Abruptly, the crowd grew silent. Ghosts on the orchestra level turned to look at the balcony, many murmuring in disbelief. A distinguished balding man with bulging, hooded eyes was making his way along the first row to a center seat.

"Who's that?" whispered Alden.

"Oh! I can't believe he's here!"

"Who is he, Julie?"

The crowd of ghosts rose to its feet. The applause was thunderous.

"This is such an honor. But he had to come—the theatre's reopening!"

"Who is it? Tell me, tell me!" Alden insisted.

"That," said Julie, "is Mr. Pantages."

Alden stared at the man in the balcony. In one of their vaudeville conversations, Walter had told her that Alexander Pantages had owned over thirty theatres in the United States and Canada. This theatre was named after him.

"They all came," Julie whispered, her eyes shining. "Every theatre ghost I've ever met or heard of is here. And they came to reopen *this* theatre. It must mean your show's gonna be successful, Alden, and the Pantages will thrive once again."

Could Julie be right? Would it mean that Alden and her mom could stay in Smithfield? She desperately hoped it could be so.

"Come on, let's go backstage," Julie said.

Julie grabbed Alden's arm and pulled her toward the alcove stairway, pushing past ghosts all exclaiming about the Pantages. They ran up the stairs and into the wings, which were bustling with backstage technicians.

"I wanna see the call-board," said Julie. "Kean put up the running order."

Alden trotted behind Julie, dodging performers in costume.

"Julie, the call-board has my mom's vaudeville show posted on it." Alden reached the end of the hall and stared at the call-board. Everything from her afternoon rehearsal was gone, replaced with ghost show details. How had they managed to do it?

"Fifteen minutes," Red called down the hallway. "Places in fifteen minutes."

"Julie?" It was Kean. "Better get into costume."

"Sure, Kean. See ya, Allie."

"Alden Proctor?" Kean asked formally. "Honored guest of the ghost vaudeville circuit, please follow me." He took her arm and ushered her into the house.

The theatre was completely empty. Confused, Alden asked Kean, "What happened to the ghosts? Hundreds of them were here a few minutes ago. Where did everyone go?"

"They're in the ballroom at a welcoming party. We couldn't let them see the final dress rehearsal. They have to wait until tomorrow night for the opening after your show. Tonight's rehearsal is entirely for you."

In the tenth row on the aisle was a seat with a red ribbon attached to the armrest.

"There you go, beautiful lady. Enjoy the vaudeville, the best entertainment in America!"

Julie had been right. The acts were spectacular. The Gleason sisters were astounding jugglers, throwing multiple bowling pins high above their heads and then passing them between each other or juggling sticks of fire, almost singeing their hair. Alden grabbed the arms of her seat during George Templeton's daring acrobatic routine on the high wire. The singers and dancers were incredible—even the dog act was hilarious! Nothing she had ever seen in New York with her grandfather was comparable.

But of all the acts, Alden was the proudest of Julie's. Her tap dance routine was exuberant, and she was flawless, her smile reaching to the back row of the theatre. Alden knew Kean was watching everything from the wings. From her special seat in the audience, she whispered, "Make Julie a headliner, Kean. Please, please make her a headliner!"

The ghosts' dress rehearsal ended, and the theatre was empty and quiet once again. Still in a daze from what she had just seen, Alden walked up the aisle and into the lobby. Dusk had settled, and the sky was laced with red sunset clouds. As she pulled open the lobby door, she caught sight of two familiar figures on the deserted outdoor mall. Taylor was arguing heatedly with Chris, her old tormentor. Alden hadn't seen Chris in months. She anxiously looked down the block in the opposite direction. There was no sign of Jewel. Alden guessed she had stuck to her promise to never come near the Pantages again and that Chris was on his own. But what was Taylor doing with Chris? And why were they arguing? Then Taylor pulled out a money clip and handed Chris what looked like several bills. Chris appeared to calm down.

Quietly, Alden let the door of the theatre close and ran down the street in the opposite direction. At the corner, she turned and looked back. Good, they hadn't seen her. Taylor and Chris shook hands, and then

Chris turned and left. Alden sprinted to the library, got on her bike, and pedaled home.

Taylor walked the half block to the Pantages and looked up at the marquee. Then he blinked his eyes and walked through the theatre wall.

18

Through the long corridors the ghosts of the past walk, unforbidden, hindered only by broken promises, dead hopes, and dream dust.

—Myrtle Reed, Old Rose and Silver

Alden arrived home after the ghost dress rehearsal to find Uncle Keller in the kitchen sampling Cleo's leftovers. Upon spying her, he hugged her and spun her around.

"Alden! You look different!" Keller exclaimed. "All grown up and as pretty as your mom."

"Stop it, Uncle Keller," Alden protested with a smile. "Everyone's excited you're the MC for our show. Mom's done so much for the theatre."

"As have you," her mom chimed in.

Alden slept late the next morning and then went to the theatre to join her mother. Prior to tomorrow night's performance, the cast would travel in costume from Locust Park to the Pantages in antique cars. Police barricades had been set up in front of the theatre on either side of an enormous red carpet leading to the lobby doors. Alden spent the morning confirming the event with the individual car owners. They would drive down Main Street—"just like the Academy Awards," she thought dreamily.

Later, she helped Walter hang the pictures they'd chosen for the historical display in the lobby.

"These pictures are the theatre's past, Alden," Walter said. "After tomorrow night's show, we'll hang pictures of the Pantages's future."

Alden hoped so.

"How was the ghost rehearsal?" he whispered to her.

"Incredible! I wish you could have seen it, Walter."

"Are you and Julie ready for *our* dress rehearsal?"

"If Julie's plan works tonight, it should work for the performance. I hope we can pull it off. She wants this so badly."

The theatre doors opened, and her mom came into the lobby with Stan, the theatre's architect.

"Would you two like to come into the theatre? We've got something to show you."

"I'll head up to the control booth," Stan said. "Shout when you're ready."

Alden and Walter followed Clare into the theatre and sat down. Clare stood in the aisle and, turning and looking up, called, "We're ready, Stan."

"Okay, Ms. Proctor, here we go!"

The house lights dimmed, and the candelabra in the niches along the outside aisle walls glowed. Alden looked up at the dome. Slowly, the stars began to twinkle on and off, while the three-dimensional white clouds glided across the blue nighttime sky. She thought of the thousands of people who'd looked up at the ceiling of the Pantages over the decades. It was inspiring.

Tears rolled down Walter's cheeks. Her mom put her hand on his shoulder.

"Thanks for making this happen, Clare. I...I...thank you."

That afternoon, Alden and her mom ordered Chinese food and ate in her office. Then they stuffed the programs with last-minute revisions, and her mom confirmed the delivery of the klieg light for tomorrow night.

Alden played with her chopsticks. Thinking ahead to the final dress rehearsal, she realized the one person who might recognize that Julie was dancing in her place was her mother.

"Mom, were you gonna watch tonight's rehearsal?"

"Of course. Why the long face? Don't you want me to come?"

"Actually, no. I want you to see it when everything's perfect. Can you wait until tomorrow for the real show?"

"I guess...if that's what you want. Greg and I can go out to dinner and pick you up afterward."

"Thanks, Mom." Alden pumped her fist under the table. One more positive step toward Julie's plan. "I'm glad you understand."

At that moment, the phone rang.

"Clare Proctor speaking. Jeremy! Are we set for the WZBS live broadcast from the theatre tomorrow night? Terrific. What? Yes, I have a TV in my office." Her mom put her hand over the mouthpiece. "Allie, turn the TV on. Sure, Jeremy. My best to Chad. See you tomorrow night."

Alden jabbed at the power button, and the screen zapped to life.

"Now, a special report." The camera zoomed in on a newswoman shuffling papers. "Good afternoon. WZBS has breaking news. State Senator, Rock Gionardi, from Michigan's sixth district will not be seeking reelection in the fall as originally expected."

"I thought he was campaigning—" Alden began.

"Shh," her mom hushed.

"This morning the Smithfield County district attorney announced that Senator Gionardi is under investigation for allegedly taking campaign contributions in return for favors to prominent Smithfield businessman, Harold Brennan."

Alden's mom clapped her hands together. "Yes!"

"Gionardi's office would not comment while the case is pending. Mr. Brennan could not be reached. In other Michigan news…"

"And Harold Brennan is taken down!" her mom declared. "Maybe my application to make the Pantages a historic landmark will finally be approved."

"Does this mean the Pantages is safe from Mr. Brennan?"

"Yes, Alden, I think it does."

The final dress rehearsal began with a whirlwind of activity. Alden peeked into the theatre. A few invited guests were starting to filter into the house. Her mother had kept her promise. She wasn't there. Alden watched the backstage hubbub of dancers warming up and stagehands making final adjustments to the scenery. Cast members jabbered in their dressing rooms, and occasional shrieks of nervous energy erupted from time to time. Keller Grant signed autographs as he studied the show's running order. Raccoon arrived, shook Walter's hand, and teasingly shoved Alden.

"Took the day off, huh?"

"I've been helping my mom!"

"Spoiled!" he ribbed.

"Hey, Raccoon," Alden said cautiously, breaking the mood. "You know Taylor, the kid in the theatre camp?"

"The one who's into you?"

"What? I never encouraged—"

"I'm just teasing," he said, cutting her off. "What about him?"

"I saw him last night, down the street from the theatre. With Chris."

"Chris…my old friend, Chris?"

"Yeah. Taylor was giving him money."

"Really?"

"How do they know each other?"

"Not sure. Forget about it, okay?"

"I guess."

"I need to check the fly rail. See ya later."

"Sure. I gotta get into costume, anyway."

Raccoon winked at her, and Alden climbed the stairs to her dressing room apprehensively. She put on her makeup and curled her hair just the way she and Julie had discussed and then put on her opening costume.

"Places, please. Places for the top of act one," called Walter.

Alden joined the rest of the cast clambering down the stairwell to the stage. As she took her place in front of the backdrop and heard the orchestra warming up, goose bumps covered her body. The music began, and the new main curtain rose into the fly loft.

The first-act rehearsal went smoothly. Artie Rosenberg stopped only a few times to fix lighting cues. At intermission, Alden ran upstairs to her dressing room and whispered, "Julie?"

She wasn't there. Anxiously, Alden changed into the beautiful costume Julie had made and put on her tap shoes and hat. Then she heard Walter call, "Five minutes until act two!"

"Julie, where are you?"

Pop! Pop! Pop! Crack! And Julie walked through the wall.

"It's about time! I was nervous that I might have to go on after all."

"Sorry. I couldn't get away from my aunts. I had to make something up."

"Make up something? Julie, what are you talking about? You mean they don't know we're doing this?"

Julie looked sheepish. "Well…"

"Gloria and Irene don't know you're dancing in my place?"

"I…I didn't want to worry them."

Alden had a dreadful thought. Was there a reason Julie hadn't told them? Was there a chance she could be exposed?

"Julie! Maybe we shouldn't—"

Walter was calling places.

Julie turned Alden toward the mirror. "See, look! Practically twins. Meet you in the alcove just before you go on." And she was gone.

Alden made her way to the wings and stood next to the rail, watching Raccoon fly the scenery in and out for the individual acts. She chewed her lip and clasped her hands, wringing them together over and over. Raccoon was watching her closely, smiling encouragingly at her.

The act before Alden's was just finishing up. She walked over to Walter and touched his arm.

"You ready?" he asked.

She nodded.

"Are you *both* ready?"

"I hope this works," she said, nodding.

"I'll distract Raccoon," Walter whispered.

Alden looked toward Raccoon. He was busy lashing off a fly rope. She slipped down the stairs and into the alcove. The light applause from the invited audience covered the cracking sound of Julie's arrival.

"This is it!" Julie said breathlessly.

Alden hugged her. "Break a leg."

Julie ran up the stairs and onto the stage. Alden leaned against the wall, her shoulders tense. She took a deep breath and moved to the edge of the alcove to watch the stage.

The conductor raised his arms, and the music began. Alden's eyes darted to the tech table set up in the middle of the audience. Artie was taking notes. Was he back far enough? Could he tell it wasn't Alden?

Julie's taps were clean with perfect execution. She was smiling brilliantly, her face lifted to the balcony. Alden's heart swelled. Julie's dream was coming true. They were pulling it off!

The number ended. Julie bowed, the stage lights blacked out, and the conductor lifted his arms to start the playoff music, when a shout came from the balcony.

"That girl isn't Alden Proctor! It's Juliette Stanton, the ghost of the Pantages!"

Chris? It was Chris's voice, Alden was sure of it. What was he doing in the theatre?

"That girl is a ghost!" he yelled again, pointing toward the dark stage.

"No!" Alden cried. He was trying to expose Julie!

Artie Rosenberg jumped into the aisle and looked up. "Who are you? What are you talking about?"

Alden could just make out Julie's silhouette on the dark stage. She was staring up at the balcony, paralyzed.

"Leave, Julie! No one can see you," Alden silently urged. "Just get out of there. That was the plan. Come on!"

Still, Julie didn't move.

Panicking, Alden whispered, "Run! Run to the alcove!"

"Juliette Stanton fell off this balcony to her death, and now she haunts this theatre. That's her tap dancing on the stage. See what happens to your vaudeville show now! No one will come see a show in a haunted theatre!"

Members of the small invited audience murmured, "That guy is nuts! He's crazy!"

Artie Rosenberg said, "Just when everything was going so well. Can somebody get that kid out of here?" Turning toward the stage, he yelled, "Can we have some house lights, please?"

Alden watched Chris's shadowy silhouette run from the balcony. Where was he going?

"Julie, get out of there!" Alden pleaded.

Finally, Julie bolted toward the wings. She reached the bottom of the stairs, her eyes huge with terror.

"Allie! I was so frightened I couldn't move. He...he's trying to expose me!"

The house lights came on, dimly spilling into the alcove. Confused voices still emanated from the audience.

Julie clutched her arm. "Alden, he knew my name. He said I was the ghost of the Pantages! Who is he?" Julie's voice trembled with fear. "I can't be exposed. I don't want to leave you or the Pantages."

"It was dark on the stage, and he was in the balcony. Maybe he couldn't see you. But you have to get out of here, now! Go!" Frantically, Alden pushed Julie toward the wall. She heard a crack, and then Julie was gone.

Bravely, Alden stepped out of the alcove and into the aisle. "What's everyone yelling about? I'm Alden Proctor."

Then she saw Chris at the back of the house. He immediately started down the aisle toward her, but suddenly an arctic blast of air blew through the theatre, and the Pantages went dark.

19

It is not length of life, but depth of life.

—Ralph Waldo Emerson

In the blackness, Alden heard yelling.

"Get the lights! Can somebody get the lights back on?"

Feeling the wall with her hands, Alden backed slowly into the alcove, inching her way up the steps and along the fly rail. She could hear Walter and Raccoon fumbling in the dark.

"I've got a flashlight here someplace," said Walter.

A beam of light shone near the podium. She ran over to them.

"Alden." Raccoon grabbed her hands. "You okay? What's going on out there?"

"I'm okay, but Raccoon, listen…" she said urgently.

"Would somebody please get the lights on?" yelled Artie Rosenberg from the audience.

"We're trying!" Walter yelled back. "The power must've gone out." He turned to Raccoon. "The breaker panel's in the basement. We've blown something. Come on."

"Raccoon, wait," urged Alden. "That person yelling from the balcony. It was Chris. He's here…in the theatre."

"Chris? What's *he* doing here?"

"Don't know."

"Listen, lemme help Walter get the lights back on, and then we'll the deal with Chris. Stay here."

"But—"

"It's okay." Raccoon placed his hand on Alden's shoulder. "I'll be right back."

"Hurry," Alden said.

Raccoon bent down and quickly kissed her cheek before running toward the backstage stairwell. She heard Walter in the hallway, yelling to the actors to stay in their dressing rooms until the lights came back on.

Alden nervously paced back and forth in the wings, her tap shoes clicking on the stage. She wanted to think about Raccoon's quick kiss but pushed it away for now. Julie's plan hadn't worked. They'd been so stupid! They never should have tried to have her perform. How did she think they could ever get away with it? Somehow, Chris knew that Julie was the ghost of the Pantages. Julie had walked through the wall after Chris had tried to ruin her, but had she disappeared in time? When she was on the stage, had the darkness of the theatre protected Julie from being exposed? Or was it too late? Alden twisted her hands together over and over. If Chris had been successful, Julie would have left the earth—and Alden would never see her again.

More yelling and commotion arose from the house. Then Alden heard footsteps in the alcove. She gripped the fly rail. A small key-chain flashlight clicked on and cast a feeble light. She could smell his breath and sweaty body. The light hit her in the face.

"Hello, Alden," said Chris.

Alden bolted toward the back hallway. Chris charged after her, knocking her to the stage, her knees slamming violently into the floor. Chris flipped her onto her back, yanked her arms roughly together, and tied them with a zip tie that cut into her wrists.

"What are you doing? Let me go!"

"Shut up," he hissed, yanking her up.

She winced in pain. "Chris, I'm obviously not a ghost, so let me go."

"Of course I know that! I only said all that stuff about the theatre being haunted because that's what I was tol' to say." Chris heaved her to her feet. "I'm getting paid to bring you to the theatre's catwalk. I want the rest of my money, so that's what I'm gonna do. Let's go." Chris grabbed her elbow and roughly pushed her in front of him.

Alden's mind reeled. Taylor had paid Chris to do this. She'd witnessed him giving Chris money on the mall. What she couldn't figure out was why.

"Lights! Lights, please!" Artie yelled from the house. "And whoever that kid is yelling all the stuff about ghosts, he's crazy. Somebody call the police."

"Help! Help me!" Alden cried, her voice cracking. But she knew no one in the house could hear her. They were too far away, and there was too much commotion.

Chris grabbed a fistful of her hair and yanked her head back.

"I told you to shut up!"

Alden pleaded again, "I'm sorry I crashed your bike last summer. Please…just let me go."

Chris steered her through the wings and then behind the backdrop, gripping her arm tightly. Even with his flashlight, she knew no one would be able to see them behind the heavy canvas. She struggled fiercely, kicking her feet at Chris. She managed to land a couple of blows to his shins, but her tap shoes didn't have the force of Jewel's combat boots. She tried reasoning with him. "You won't get away with this. Raccoon will be back any minute. Just let me go."

Chris grunted and shoved her up the spiral staircase. The yelling in the theatre was louder now. Her taps clanged on the metal steps, inaudible to anyone else.

As they reached the top, Chris pushed her shoulders with both hands. Alden stumbled onto the catwalk, the cord around her wrists digging into her skin. What was Chris planning on doing with her? Alden began shaking uncontrollably, her teeth chattering. She looked around wildly for a way to escape.

Glancing down, she saw a large flashlight beam sweeping the stage thirty feet below them. Chris saw it, too. He pushed her down onto her knees and cupped his hand over her mouth.

"Not a word," he whispered into her ear.

"Alden?" yelled Raccoon. "Where are you?" Raccoon's voice was raspy with panic.

Alden bit down hard on Chris's fingers, and he cried out, shaking his bleeding hand.

"Raccoon! Help me!"

"Alden? Walter, somebody's got Alden! Alden, where are you?"

"I told you to shut up!" Chris slapped Alden's face sharply. She screamed and fell backward, the side of her head striking the metal railing. Pain exploded behind her eyes.

Agonizingly, Alden pushed herself onto her knees and inched along the catwalk away from Chris. Blood ran into her mouth. She fought to calm her nausea.

Chris charged forward and shoved her. Alden rolled toward the side of the catwalk, teetering near the edge. Alden reached up desperately with her bound hands, clawed at the railing, and wrapped her fingers around it. Terrified, she waited for Chris's next blow.

Instead, a green orb of light illuminated itself and landed on the catwalk. After a moment, the orb dissipated, materializing into the human persona of Taylor, standing where the light had been.

"Holy shit!" Chris cried out.

"I'll take it from here, Chris," Taylor said.

"But...but..." Chris stammered.

Stunned, Alden struggled to comprehend what she now realized was true. Taylor was a ghost. The ghost she hadn't met. The one who'd somehow infiltrated himself into the theatre camp and gained her trust. Julie had told her the disgruntled ghost was the son of Mr. Pantages! Taylor McCord Pantages!

"Taylor, help me, please!" Alden whimpered.

"Save the girl who wants to save the Pantages? I don't think so. You got the better of me the first time you got all your friends to come to the rescue. Not this time. This theatre will never reopen. And you, my lovely dancer, are about to disappear from the earth and become a ghost...like me." Slowly he walked toward Alden, his eyes narrowed into slits.

"I thought we were friends."

"Joke's on you. I'm a magician, but I'm also a good actor."

With a scream of outrage, Taylor shoved his foot into Alden's side and pushed. Her body rolled off the catwalk. High above the stage, Alden's legs flailed in the open air. She was still gripping the catwalk railing, but her hands were starting to slip. No! She didn't want to die. She didn't want to become a ghost of the Pantages. She wasn't ready to join them. Desperately, she hung on.

"Help!" Alden screamed.

"Alden!" yelled Raccoon. "Walter, she's on the catwalk. We're coming, Alden!"

Alden wasn't sure she could hold on long enough for Raccoon to reach her. Her grip was fading, her fingers weakening…

Just when she thought she couldn't hold on any longer, a purple orb burst through the wall behind Taylor, zoomed past his ear, and landed on the catwalk next to her. The orb of light materialized. In the semidarkness, Alden smelled peppermint. Just as her body was about to plummet to the stage, a strong hand grasped her arm.

"I gotcha, Miss Alden."

Red pulled her up onto the catwalk and steadied her trembling body. He took an army knife out of his pocket and, using his teeth, flipped it open and quickly cut the zip ties on her wrists.

"Get behind me, Alden," Red warned.

"What the hell am I seeing?" cried Chris from the end of the catwalk, his face ashen in the dim glow of his flashlight. Alden had momentarily forgotten he was there. She heard pounding on the spiral stairs and Raccoon yelling her name.

"This is insane, Taylor! The girl's done nothing to you." Red's normally gravelly voice was bitter with anger.

"Stay out of this, Red."

Red stepped closer to Taylor, his one arm stretched in front of him, his eyes watching him warily.

"You know what will happen if we battle," Taylor warned.

"I know," Red answered.

"No!" Alden cried.

Instantly, Red and Taylor's human forms turned into green and purple circles of light. The two orbs charged toward each other and collided just above Alden's head. There was a blaze of color—violent bolts of purple and green—and the sound of static energy was loud in her ears.

"Red!" Alden yelled.

The colors fought to absorb each other, first green and then purple, back and forth until there was no dominant color, just a blazing light. Then, with an explosion that shook the catwalk, the combined crashing orbs shattered into translucent specks of light, each speck dying out as they drifted slowly to the stage.

"Nooooo!" Alden cried. The theatre was silent after the battle.

Chris shook his head in disbelief. "Who were those people, those… those things?"

Alden dragged her eyes from the falling bits of glowing light and stared into Chris's shocked face. She raised her chin in a gesture reminiscent of Raccoon's.

"What are you talking about? I didn't see anybody."

"You…you were just talking to Taylor and…and a man. He had one arm. They were here. There was bright light, and now they're gone."

"You're seeing things."

Chris lunged threateningly toward Alden just as Raccoon and Walter reached the top of the stairs. Alden's eyes darted toward Raccoon. Chris whirled around to face him.

"Leave her alone, Chris."

"There are ghosts in this theatre!" Chris yelled.

"That's crazy." Raccoon edged slowly out onto the catwalk. "The cops are coming, Chris. Make it easy on yourself."

"No, seriously, there're ghosts here." Chris was wild eyed, his face mixed with confusion and fear. "I just saw them disappear into thin air!"

Raccoon's voice was calm, reassuring. "There's no such thing as ghosts, dude, and people don't just vanish. Listen, man, you need help."

A police siren outside the theatre pierced the silence. Chris's eyes zigzagged back and forth along the catwalk. Violently, he pushed past Alden, ran toward the fire door, threw it open, and clanged down the fire escape.

Alden stumbled to Raccoon, throwing her arms around his waist.

"Allie!" His voice broke as he wrapped his arms around her. She buried her face in his chest and wept.

20

Look not mournfully into the past. It comes not back again. Wisely improve the present. It is thine. Go forth to meet the shadowy future, without fear.

—HENRY WADSWORTH LONGFELLOW

Alden drifted in and out of sleep. She was running through a dark hallway. People were yelling. Someone was chasing her. Her tap shoes were clanging on metal. Red was gone, and Taylor was evil. Where was Julie? Julie, are you still among us, or were you exposed?

Alden dragged herself out of intense grogginess and slowly focused on the cheerful yellow walls of her bedroom. Her head throbbed. Reaching up, she felt a bandage on her head.

Last night, her mom and Greg had insisted on taking her to the hospital to make sure she didn't have a concussion. The doctor released her and told her to get some rest. Rest! Last night, she didn't think she'd ever sleep again. But when her mother had tucked her comforter under her chin, she'd instantly fallen asleep.

Her mom now tiptoed into the room. Greg was leaning against the doorframe, his dark eyes full of concern. Alden noted her mother's ashen face.

"You look awful."

"I know, right? I never went to sleep." Her mom sat down on her bed. "Alden, if anything had happened to you…"

Alden sat up and hugged her. They held each other, not speaking, just rocking back and forth.

"The police caught Chris. They're looking for Taylor, but he seems to have gotten away. Chris has been admitted to a psychiatric hospital for observation and treatment. He was raving something about ghosts and the Pantages being haunted. Can you imagine? Ghosts!"

"Hard to believe," said Alden softly.

"Raccoon's here. He slept on the couch. He insisted on staying, so I called his uncle and made something up about there being a late rehearsal. And Alden, Artie Rosenberg thinks we should postpone the show."

Alden pulled away. "No. He can't. We have to do the show!"

"I'm not sure, Alden. Maybe Artie is right. First the theatre was vandalized, and now this. A crime was committed last night. You were abducted, and you could have been killed. If it hadn't been for Raccoon…" Her voice trembled.

"We have to do the show tonight, Mom! Everyone's worked so hard. Please…what would Grandpa have done?"

Her mom managed a weak smile and met Alden's passionate gaze. "He'd have gone ahead with the show." She looked over at Greg and then back at Alden. "All right, I'll talk to Artie—but the doctor said you should take it easy."

"I'm going on tonight, Mom. I have to!"

"You've got a lot of my father in you, Alden, my girl," her mom said, sighing. She patted Alden's hand. "I'll make us some breakfast. Cleo is catering the cast party at Winkie's tonight, so I gave her the day off." She kissed Greg on her way out the door.

"Hey," Greg said, watching her warily. "Can I come in?"

"Sure."

"How are you feeling?"

"A little sore."

Greg looked out the window and said softly, "I'm sure glad you're okay." He raked his hand through his hair. "We should have been there last night…at the rehearsal."

"It's not your fault. I didn't want you to see the show until the opening."

"I know, but…"

Alden patted the bed next to her. "I'm okay, Greg."

"Thankfully, yes." Greg relaxed next to her and said, "I want to show you something."

He pulled a small velvet box out of his pocket and handed it to Alden. She snapped it open. A brilliant diamond ring glistened in the box.

"Oh, Greg, it's beautiful!"

"Um…obviously it's for your mom. I wanted to see how you felt about it before I asked her."

Alden threw her arms around him. "Ask her tonight, before the show!" Alden said excitedly. "And I know exactly where you should sit in the theatre. Lemme get your tickets, okay?"

"Does it matter where our seats are?"

"Yes, it does! Trust me."

"Okay," said Greg, laughing.

With every minute that passed, the day was improving. Alden ran downstairs to see Raccoon.

At dusk, the cast gathered in Locust Park. They were dressed in costumes from the 1920s. Alden, Raccoon, the Friedman Twins, Garrett, and Melody were seated in a large antique touring automobile. Garrett could barely control himself.

"This car is sweet!"

A soft breeze blew off the lake. The moon was a perfect sliver surrounded by hundreds of stars, while a few wistful clouds moved gently toward the moon. "Just like the dome of the theatre," Alden thought.

The preshow parade to the Pantages pulled onto Main Street. Clare, Walter, and Keller rode in the lead car. As they drew closer to the theatre, the cheering crowds behind the police barricades grew louder. Alden couldn't stop grinning.

"How's the head?" Raccoon asked.

"I'm fine." Her head hurt, but nothing was going to keep her from performing tonight.

"Look!" yelled Jenna, pointing up. Klieg lights swept back and forth across the dark sky. "They're coming from the roof of the Pantages!"

Television cameramen were filming the parade. "Reporting live from the Pantages Theatre for WZBS—the event Smithfield has been waiting for…"

The reporter continued on as Alden sucked in a huge gulp of air and thought of her Grandpa Charlie. As much as she missed him, Alden was content that he wasn't a theatre ghost—stuck and earthbound. In her heart, she knew he had moved on to the spiritual world because he had passed his love of the theatre on to her. Her Grandpa Charlie would always be with her and be a part of her. Theatre was in her blood. "Oh, Grandpa," she whispered. "The show's gonna be a hit."

Alighting in front of the theatre, Alden walked down the red carpet toward the double doors as flashbulbs blinded her, and then she slipped into the box office.

"Hi, Mrs. Waters."

"Hello, Alden."

"Did you get the tickets?"

"Here you go. Break legs tonight."

"Thanks." Spotting Greg in the lobby, she ran over to him. "Here ya go. Row J, seats 101 and 102. Guaranteed she'll say yes."

Greg's blue eyes looked fondly into hers. "I hope so, hon." As Alden started toward the theatre doors, he added, "Hey, Alden? Knock 'em dead."

Alden pumped her fist and headed backstage. Outside her dressing room, she heard four distinctive cracks from inside. Nervously, Alden looked back down the hallway. It was empty. She slowly pushed open the door.

The Gleason sisters, Kean, and Julie were waiting for her. Quickly, she closed and locked the door behind her.

"Julie!" A wave of relief overcame her as she stumbled toward Julie. "You're okay? You weren't exposed?

"No. I'm still a ghost." Julie twisted her dress in her hands. "The black-out after my dance routine saved me. Gloria and Irene explained to me that an Alive has to look directly at you in order to expose you." Pausing, Julie met Alden's eyes. "I'm so ashamed, Allie. Not only did I risk my ghost life, but you could have been killed by that monster Chris."

"I'm alive because of Red. He saved me." At the thought of Red, tears spilled onto Alden's cheeks.

Gloria was crying along with Alden. "We know, dear. He insisted he was the ghost to battle Taylor."

Alden swallowed. "He…he crossed over into the spiritual world, didn't he? He sacrificed himself to help me."

Kean spoke up, his voice gruff with pain. "Yes, he did. But he knew what he was doing. He wanted to save your life."

"I'll miss him," Alden whispered. They were silent for a moment. "So Taylor wasn't a camp student after all. He was the other ghost who lived here?"

"The son of old Mr. Pantages," Kean answered.

"But why did he hate this theatre so much?"

"His father never believed Taylor's magic act was good enough for the circuit and only allowed him to be Marco the Knife Thrower's apprentice. Plus, he was embarrassed to have had a son out of wedlock and never fully accepted him as his own. All this infuriated Taylor. It's why he used his mother's maiden name, McCord, instead of Pantages. And he warned us…" Kean glanced over at the Gleason sisters, "*all* of us, that Marco was drinking heavily." Gloria and Irene nodded, guilt etched on their faces. "I should have listened. Mr. Pantages should have listened. We foolishly ignored his warnings about Marco. Then, one night, Taylor was struck by a wildly thrown knife and was killed."

Even though Taylor had tried to kill her, Alden felt some compassion for him. "How awful."

"After he became a theatre ghost," Kean continued, "Taylor blamed his father. He vowed that the Pantages would close and that no one would ever perform on its stage again. Unfortunately, after vaudeville died, the Pantages hit hard times, and the theatre did shut down. Taylor withdrew from the ghost world completely."

"But why would he want to harm *me*?" Alden asked.

Kean ran his hand through his hair. "You and your mom and what you've been trying to do here were a threat to him and his vow. He was determined to stop you. First, he chose to show himself to all the theatre kids, which was incredibly reckless. Then he befriended you, hoping to gain your trust and keep you from discovering his secret. He thought the damage he'd done to the theatre and the warnings to you and your mom would scare you into quitting and moving back to New York. But you weren't about to quit. You were so courageous, Alden, that *you* became the problem. You became what he had to eliminate."

Alden shivered. The terror of almost falling from the catwalk was still too close. She glanced around. The sewing machine was gone. Only one yellow dress with peach flowers hung on the costume rack. The ghosts were silent, watching her.

After a moment, Gloria said sternly, "When Julie told us what happened and what you two had been planning for months, we were appalled. If we'd known, you two would never have been allowed to go through with this."

"Alden, will you ever forgive me?" asked Julie.

"Of course," she said, hugging her tightly.

"You'll dance tonight, Alden," Julie said proudly. "I know you never thought it would turn out this way, but you're ready."

"I was pretty irresponsible when I was Julie's age," admitted Kean, ruffling Julie's hair. "I guess it's part of growing up—even in death," he said glibly. "Besides, Julie's going to be too busy to get herself into trouble again."

Julie looked curiously at Kean, and he flashed her his dazzling grin. "I'm making you a headliner." Julie gasped and let out a screech. "You, Juliette Stanton, will headline the ghost vaudeville show. Tonight, the Pantages—next week, the entire West Coast!"

Julie's face was radiant.

"Half hour! Half hour, everyone!" Walter called from the hallway. "We're sold out, folks. Half hour."

"Gotta go," Kean said, tipping his hat. Gloria and Irene touched Alden's cheek, and then they all walked through the wall.

"Break a leg, Allie," Julie whispered, "you're gonna be fantastic." And then she was gone as well.

"Alden?" Walker knocked softly.

Alden blinked away tears and opened the door.

"How's the injured dancer?"

"I'm fine."

"And Julie?"

"She wasn't exposed. She escaped just in time."

"You've got a lot of grit, kid, insisting we go ahead with the show tonight after what you've been through." Walter's old eyes crinkled up. "So…you ready to go on?"

"Yup."

"Nervous?"

"No, I'm not." Alden looked into Walter's kind face. "I'm gonna use the energy of the Pantages."

"Thatta girl."

Unlike the audition, Alden remembered every moment of the show. The elation she felt when the curtain rose on the opening number, the camaraderie of dancing with the other chorus members, the thrill of dancing her filler act and hearing the applause afterward, and finally the realization that she was now a part of a tight-knit, brave group. She was a theatre kid.

Afterward, Alden stood in the wings, dressed for the cast party. Shouts of congratulations echoed in her ears. It was over. The main curtain had come down to cries of "Bravo! Bravo!" along with "Long live the Pantages!" During the curtain call, she saw her mother applauding, the diamond ring sparkling on her left hand. As Alden listened to the applause, her eyes swept over the orchestra and then lifted to the balcony. She didn't think she had ever been so happy.

Just then, Raccoon came up behind her. He slipped his arms around her waist and pressed against her. Alden relaxed against his body. She wasn't self-conscious this time. It felt right.

"You were wonderful tonight."

Alden turned in his arms. "Thanks. I…" Alden swallowed and looked up at him. "I like you, Raccoon. I like you a lot. I was afraid to tell you before. But I'm not now."

Raccoon brushed her hair away from her face and rubbed the back of his fingers along her cheek. "I like you a lot, too."

Alden reached up and touched his lips with her fingertips. He kissed each finger one by one, and then he bent down and kissed her on the lips. As he gently pulled away, he said, "Your mom and Greg are waiting in the alley. I guess we should hit the party."

"In a minute. Would you mind going to Winkie's with them? I'll come with Walter in a little bit."

"Sure. Take your time." Alden put her arms around Raccoon's neck and pulled his mouth down to hers. After a while, Raccoon pulled away with a grin.

"Keep that up, and I'll wanna stay here." Reluctantly, he left through the stage door.

Alden's eyes roamed the wings, taking in the fly rail, the lighting control panel, the curtains, and the fly loft. She was proud. Proud of her mother, proud of herself. They had moved to Smithfield almost a year ago. The Pantages was Julie's home, and Smithfield was now Alden's.

Walter left the archive room and quietly entered the wings, lovingly watching Alden. "It's happening tonight, isn't it? The ghost show?"

Alden nodded.

"I think you should do the honors," Walter said. Alden looked at him, tears brimming in her eyes. "It's all set to go. You know what to do. I'll wait for you in the alley."

Alden walked out onto the stage and looked at the sea of red seats. She knew they were all there. Olive Thomas in her beaded green gown, surrounded by adoring admirers; Mr. Belasco in his priestly garb, sitting stoically in the theatre box; Ray Bolger and Harpo Marx joking with the crowd; and Mr. Pantages in his seat of honor.

She knew the performers were in the dressing rooms, putting on their costumes. Musicians were warming up in the pit, and dancers were stretching and going over their routines. Gloria and Irene would be happily putting on their makeup, while Kean, patiently placating George Templeton's latest complaints, would simultaneously flirt with the chorus girls. And Juliette Stanton was the new headliner. The stage manager would call places, and there would be a communal rush of adrenaline.

Her mother's show tonight had guaranteed the reopening of the theatre. Pictures of tonight's event would join others in the lobby, beginning a new chapter in the theatre's history. But Alden knew their show tonight was only an imitation of what it used to be. The *real* show was about to begin. The Pantages Theatre was about to rejoin the vaudeville ghost circuit.

Smiling, Alden walked to the lighting panel, reached up, and pulled down the main lever. The stage was blanketed in darkness, except for one light—the ghost light that would bring the real stars to the stage.

Acknowledgments

I would like to thank the hundreds of theatre students I have taught over the past twenty-five years for inspiring many of the characters in this story.

For their hours of encouragement and input, my heartfelt appreciation goes out to Nancy Auffarth, Michael Berkeley, Laurie Bryant, Pamela Chassin, Bill and Marie Combs, Mary Carol Combs, Dorothy Conley, Ellen Crimmins, Erik and Holly Diaz, Caitlin Dougherty Duffy, Jonathan Gaughan, Jenna Karn, Grace Mihalchik, Lucille Ogden, Sean Petersen, Rio Reilly, John Rosegrant, and all my reading partners at Shop Talk Poughkeepsie.

Thanks also to Chris Woodyard for allowing me to use her quote, originally published at hauntedohiobooks.com, which is used by permission of Kestrel Publications, copyright @ 1990–2000 Chris Woodyard.

Lastly, my life would not be complete without Rich and Jamie. Thank you for your love, laughter, and applause.

A final shout-out to the theatre legends who have inspired me to pursue not only theatre, theatre history, and vaudeville but also writing about it for young people. I want to thank the ghosts and specters who have populated theatres across the country, including *Ziegfeld Follies* girl Olive Thomas, who haunts the New Amsterdam Theatre in NYC; David Belasco (a.k.a. the Bishop of B-Way) of the Belasco Theatre on Forty-Fourth Street in NYC; and One-Armed Red, who posthumously graced the stage of the Lincoln Square Theatre in Decatur, Illinois. Some of the characters in *Theatre Ghost* are modeled after these colorful individuals.

If readers are interested in exploring the history of these individuals and the theatres they haunted, here are two useful sources, including both books and websites:

Lewis, Roy Harley. *Theatre Ghosts*. Vermont, USA: David & Charles Inc, 1988.

Viagas, Robert. "Scandals and Secrets of the Supernatural: The Stories Behind Broadway's Haunted Theatres." Playbill.com. Last modified October 30, 2014.

https://www.playbill.com/article/scandals-and-secrets-of-the-super-natural-the-stories-behind-broadways-haunted-theatres-com-334137.

In addition, do you want to know more about the theatres or ghosts mentioned? Here is a list of all the interesting characters and places Alden references that really existed or are rumored to exist.

David Belasco—"The Bishop of Broadway." His ghost is rumored to haunt his namesake theatre on West Forty-Fourth Street in New York City.

Jack Benny (1894–1974)—vaudeville comedian.

Ray Bolger (1904–1987)—vaudeville entertainer.

The Fox Theatre—Atlanta, Georgia.

Lincoln Square Theatre—Decatur, Illinois. Rumored to be the home of ghost One-Armed Red.

Harpo Marx (1888–1964)—Comedian and a member of the Marx Brothers' family comedy act.

The New Amsterdam Theatre—Forty-Second Street, New York City.

Olive Thomas—a *Ziegfeld Follies* girl who haunts the New Amsterdam Theatre.

The Palace Theatre—the pinnacle of vaudeville in its day. Rumored to be the home of over one hundred ghosts.

Alexander Pantages (1867–1936)—an American vaudeville producer who owned a large circuit of theatres across the western United States and Canada.

Radio City Music Hall—Sixth Avenue, New York City.

Vaudeville—a type of theatrical entertainment. It was especially popular in the United States and Canada from the early 1880s until the early 1930s.

Florenz Ziegfeld Jr. (1867–1932)—Broadway impresario and producer of the *Ziegfeld Follies*.

Sarah A. Combs worked as a professional actress for a decade, including starring in off-Broadway productions, regional theatre, and daytime dramas, before focusing her attention on teaching drama to high school youth, which she has done—along with directing—for over twenty-five years. She is a member of the Actors' Equity Association and a theatre director. She attended the Cincinnati Conservatory of Music, where she received her BFA in musical theatre performance, and she also has an MA in theatre education. Sarah believes theatre education is an essential part of the high school curriculum. She is on the board of directors of the Sharon Playhouse in Sharon, Connecticut and a member of the New York State Theatre Education Association.

Sarah resides in New York's Hudson Valley with her husband. She has one son, who is a lighting designer based in New York City. *Theatre Ghost* is her first novel.

Theatre Ghost is loosely based on the State Theatre, an old vaudeville house in Kalamazoo, Michigan, that was slated to be demolished in the early 1980s. Local arts groups and city officials, including Sarah, formed the "Save the State" committee in an effort to preserve the theatre. The State Theatre still exists today because of that effort.

The State Theatre in Kalamazoo, Michigan
Photograph by Mark Cassino
www.markcassino.com

61937936R00090

Made in the USA
Lexington, KY
24 March 2017